CAUGHT IN THE MIDDLE

They came at my partner, and I got caught in the middle. I'd been through enough that day and was ready to fight. But it was nearly impossible being chained to somebody. It was like two sets of Siamese twins trying to beat on each other, only that other pair was working with the same brain.

Before I got hit, I saw the spiderweb tattoo on one of their necks and the light reflecting off the burner in his hand. I threw my arms up, swinging back as hard as I could. Then I felt the side of my face get warm, and I tried to touch it with my cuffed hands.

The two of them jumped back into the crowd of inmates. I tried to go after them, but I got pushed down by COs.

I could feel the blood between my cheek and the ground.

The tattooed kid had cut me across the face with a razor.

The sharp sting started to pulse high on my cheek. Then it went racing down my entire body, like I'd been sliced from head to toe. Suddenly, I was paralyzed with fear, and I was too shook to even cry.

BOOKS BY PAUL VOLPONI

Black and White
Crossing Lines
Hurricane Song
Rikers High
Rooftop
Rucker Park Setup

PAUL VOLPONI

speak

An Imprint of Penguin Group (USA) Inc.

SPEAK
Published by the Penguin Group
Penguin Group (USA) Inc., 345 Hudson Street, New York, New York 10014, U.S.A.
Penguin Group (Canada), 90 Eglinton Avenue East, Suite 700, Toronto, Ontario, Canada M4P 2Y3
(a division of Pearson Penguin Canada Inc.)
Penguin Books Ltd, 80 Strand, London WC2R 0RL, England
Penguin Ireland, 25 St Stephen's Green, Dublin 2, Ireland (a division of Penguin Books Ltd)
Penguin Group (Australia), 250 Camberwell Road, Camberwell, Victoria 3124, Australia
(a division of Pearson Australia Group Pty Ltd)
Penguin Books India Pvt Ltd, 11 Community Centre, Panchsheel Park, New Delhi - 110 017, India
Penguin Group (NZ), 67 Apollo Drive, Rosedale, North Shore 0632, New Zealand
(a division of Pearson New Zealand Ltd.)
Penguin Books (South Africa) (Pty) Ltd, 24 Sturdee Avenue,
Rosebank, Johannesburg 2196, South Africa

Registered Offices: Penguin Books Ltd, 80 Strand, London WC2R 0RL, England

Published in slightly different form as *Rikers* in 2002 by Black Heron Press.

This edition first published in 2010 by Viking, a member of Penguin Group (USA) Inc.

Published by Speak, an imprint of Penguin Group (USA) Inc., 2011

5 7 9 10 8 6 4

Copyright © Paul Volponi, 2002, 2010
All rights reserved

THE LIBRARY OF CONGRESS HAS CATALOGED THE VIKING EDITION AS FOLLOWS:
Volponi, Paul.
Rikers High / by Paul Volponi.
p. cm.
Originally published in 2002 in slightly different form
by Black Heron Press under title: Rikers.
Summary: Arrested on a minor offense, a New York City teenager attends high school
in the jail facility on Rikers Island, as he waits for his case to go to court.
ISBN: 978-0-670-01107-0 (hc)
[1. Jails—Fiction. 2. Prisoners—Fiction. 3. Juvenile delinquency—Fiction.
4. Rikers Island (N.Y.)—Fiction. 5. African Americans—Fiction.]
I. Volponi, Paul. Rikers. II. Title.
PZ7.V8877Ri 2010
[Fic]—dc22
2009022471

Speak ISBN 978-0-14-241778-2

Printed in the United States of America
Set in Palatino
Book design by Sam Kim

This text is dedicated to all of the high school students behind bars. Students who face the types of pressures that would break most adults, yet still find the strength to be concerned about moving forward with their education, for themselves and their families.

Special thanks to Joy Peskin, Regina Hayes, Rosemary Stimola, Jim Cocoros, David Addison, Tyrone Thompson, April Volponi, Mary Volponi, and Sabrina Volponi.

AUTHOR'S NOTE:

The overwhelming majority of incidents that occur in this book really happened. I witnessed them firsthand during the six years I worked as a teacher on Rikers Island. The fiction here is the creation of a protagonist who represents the actual experiences of several student-inmates.

TUESDAY, JUNE 2

CHAPTER
1

Every morning at five o'clock another correction officer came on duty and started to count. For five months it had been the same. One of them would drive in from someplace nice, like Long Island, while another went home. The one coming on would start down the row of beds, counting, before he could steal an hour or two of sleep in the Plexiglas bubble—their little command center at the front of our module.

They can't take the count by looking. Just like in the movies, a kid could roll his clothes up under a blanket and be on the loose. So they count by feeling for a warm body.

There's nothing worse than waking up when a CO touches you. For a second, you might not remember where you are. You might even think you're home. Then it all comes rushing back into your brain. You're on Rikers Island. To fall asleep again is like spending another night in jail.

"Thirty-six . . . thirty-seven . . . thirty-eight," the CO muttered.

The new jack next to me had spent the night before fighting off the wolves for his good kicks. He didn't know the routine yet, and wasn't ready for anyone to touch him while he was still asleep.

"Who's that?" he screamed, jumping up in his bed.

"Yo, thirty-nine!" the CO shot back, pinning his shoulders to the mattress. "I'm just takin' the count, kid. Grab a fuckin' hold of yourself!"

It seemed like half the house was awake for a few seconds, until they saw it was nothing.

"Forty, court!" the officer hollered, and shook me with one hand.

I was going to court this morning. I got my best clothes—my cleanest jeans and collared polo shirt—from the plastic bucket under my bed. Then I got dressed in the dark.

I didn't tell anyone I expected to go home. Some inmates will start trouble with you because they're jealous or think you won't fight back and chance getting a new charge. The ones you owe from juggling commissary will want to settle right away. Anyone who owes *you* will put it off, hoping you don't come back from court. And the sneak thieves will be looking for your blanket and what's left of your commissary and clothes before your bed gets cold.

I walked up to the bubble where the COs sit, and I got in line with the other courts. A CO pulled my ID card from the box and threw it on top of the pile of black and brown faces. It read, "Martin Stokes—Adolescent Reception and Detention Center, Mod-3, North Side #40." I had been answering to "Forty" for so long, it was almost like that was really my name. I would only hear "Martin" when I called home, or when Mom came on a visit.

The picture stapled to the corner of the card was taken my first day on the Island, two weeks before I turned seventeen. I thought I'd be here for a hot minute then. It was such a bubble-gum charge. I thought Mom could make my $5,000 bail, or I'd get a program and probation when I got to court. But my case was put off twice for bullshit.

First, my lawyer had to tell the judge we weren't ready. Then the judge got held up on another case. Now it had been five months since I was out in the world, and I was hungry to see it again without peeping through a chain-link fence.

There was a bang at the steel door to our mod.

It was a woman CO who'd come to collect me and four other kids. We eyeballed her up and down. She was pretty enough. But women don't have to look too good in jail to get a lot of attention. Most times, inmates, especially adolescents, are just happy to be anywhere near one. Only I was thinking more about Mom, and getting a chance to see my little sisters, Trisha and Tina, and Grandma again.

We deuced it up in the hall, getting into two lines. That woman CO had inmates from other houses out there, and we were already mixing with adults, who have their own modules.

Then she marched us down the main corridor. Except for other officers standing their posts, it was totally empty. And with the sun coming up behind those barred windows, I started to think about how it's almost peaceful on Rikers that early in the morning, when the only movement through the halls are the courts.

CHAPTER

We got to the yard, and I was shackled to another inmate by my foot and wrist, so it would be that much harder for either of us to run. They loaded us onto a blue and white bus with the word CORRECTION painted on the side. Like people on the streets wouldn't figure it out from the metal bars and plates on the windows. Then the bus started up, and we passed through the big gates and over the bridge that separates Rikers Island from the world.

There were fourteen pairs of inmates shackled together and two officers along for the ride. One CO stays with the inmates, and the driver sits on the other side of the bars so no one can take control of the bus. There's even a cage that the CO can lock you up in if you start trouble or need protection. The mood on the way to court is usually pretty good. But the ride back can be long and hard if enough dudes get smacked down by the judges.

We crossed the bridge and were on the streets of East Elmhurst. It felt good to see people walking in any direction they wanted, without a CO to stop them. And I wanted to be that way again, too.

I saw a man picking up after his dog on a corner, and I thought about my first trip to the Island. Maybe I was ten years old then. Mom took me on a visit with her to see Pops on Rikers. But we got off some city bus and couldn't find the jail.

She stopped a white man walking a black Rottweiler and asked, "How do you get to Rikers Island?"

The man just laughed and said, "Rob a bank, lady. Rob a bank."

I know where the Island is *now*. I know the bus route from the jail to the Queens Criminal Courthouse and back. I've taken that ride so many times on this one case, I could close my eyes and tell you where the bus is by the bumps and turns. From the streets to the Grand Central Parkway, through the exit ramp and the turn onto Queens Boulevard, I could feel it in my bones.

At the courthouse, we were put into the pens. You pick up a lot of skills in jail, and in the pens you need them all. The pens are big cells, with maybe fifty inmates inside of each one. That's where everybody waits until their case gets called. There's an open toilet, a sink, and benches bolted to the floor so nobody throws them. The COs in charge aren't interested in what you do because they don't have to live with you for long. They don't really want to come inside and stop anything,

either. It's up to you to take care of yourself. As long as you
come out in one piece to see the judge, they did their job.

Adolescents are mixed with adults in the pens, and guys
that fly the same colors stay together and act tight. By eleven
o'clock, the COs serve you a slice of bologna between two
pieces of bread for lunch. Inmates call them "cop-out sand-
wiches" because you'd be willing to confess to anything just to
not eat that crap. After a while, the floor of the pen gets covered
with bologna and stale bread.

I tried to look hard, with my chest puffed out and eyes
squinting. I was as worried about the next few hours as I was
about my case.

Some guys had bullied a weak kid over in the corner into
doing the pogo—jumping up and down in the toilet on one
foot in his shoes and socks. It's mostly the adolescents who do
stuff like that because they want to show other kids how tough
they are. The only time an adult will step to an adolescent is if
the kid is acting real stupid. And when adults fight, there's no
playing around. They'll pull burners quick and try to stab each
other to death.

The dude standing next to me was practicing hand signs,
and I thought he was down with one of the gangs. He saw me
watching him and said, "This is what's gonna help me beat my
case."

Then he ran down the whole show for me.

"All the judges are Masons," he said. "If they see you
throwing up the right signs, they won't find you guilty. That's

why you don't see white people going through the system. Most of them are Masons, and they know the signs. But there are black Masons, too. Even a white judge knows that."

I just nodded. You never want to argue with a dude when he has his hopes riding on something crazy like that. Not while he's waiting to see the judge and is all uptight.

There were two kids starting to jaw in the corner of the pen. They were fighting over which outfit ran their neighborhood, and it was starting to get heavy. They both had on their best ice grills, and one of them had backup.

"You're talkin' to me like I'm some sort of punk," said the one standing alone.

He put his fists up and stood with his back to the bars, so no one could yoke him from behind. But that crew had him surrounded and other inmates in that part of the pen started to move away.

It was about to be high drama when an officer came up to the bars and shouted, "All right boys and *girls*, listen up! Fuller, Douglas, Stokes, and Wallace, let's go!"

"That's me, Martin Stokes," I told the officer, as his key rattled the lock on the door.

CHAPTER

I hadn't seen my legal aid lawyer since the last time I went to court, fifty-one days ago. I'd called her plenty since then, and so did Mom. But she was never there and wouldn't get back to us. That happened so many times we got to know the message on her answering machine by heart and would tear it to pieces on visits.

"I'm either in court right now or on the phone. Leave your name and case number, and I'll get back to you as soon as possible."

One time, I just screamed "Forty!" into the phone and hung up.

I'd only met her five minutes before I saw the judge on my first trip to court. Until she said my name, I had no idea she was my lawyer. She was young and black, and I thought she was the girl or sister of somebody on trial. Then I noticed the briefcase in her hand.

"My name is Gale Thompson," she said, inside of a small conference room. "I've been assigned to represent you in this matter."

Before she even asked me what happened, she started to explain how I was guilty and what kind of deal she could get me.

They had me for "steering"—telling an undercover cop where to buy weed in my neighborhood. I told her I did it, but that it was really a setup. How the dude who walked up to me was diesel, and I was afraid not to tell him anything or he might start to beef with me. I told her that she had to tell my side of it, too, before I got anywhere near calling myself guilty.

We argued back and forth for a while. Then she just threw her hands up and sent a note to the judge saying we weren't ready. He didn't like that, and I had to wait almost ten weeks to come back. That's when I thought Mom would do anything to make my bail. But she didn't have the money and had to worry about supporting my sisters and Grandma.

I didn't see Miss Thompson again until the next time my case came up.

"I hope you're through with all that nonsense and we can get down to the business of getting you home," she said. "I've got a lot of cases to handle, and this one is cut and dry."

By then I'd seen lots of kids go home on more serious charges. I just wanted to be done with jail and to get my ass out of this stinking parade. So I kept my mouth shut. But the judge got caught up in some case that went to trial, and I never even made it into the courtroom that day.

Now I was glad to see Miss Thompson. I was happy to get out of the pen before it exploded and finally go home. The CO took me to a side room where she was sitting at a table, studying her papers.

"I've arranged for you to go home and get off this public support." she said. "The assistant DA has agreed to probation, but the judge is out sick and we have to come back in a couple of weeks, on the nineteenth."

My brain just shut down for a second, and it was like I was frozen stiff.

I couldn't believe it. I was going back to Rikers Island.

Couldn't they get another judge? Couldn't the DA just send me home?

I was tired of getting shuffled around, and she was the only one in the room to hear it. So I started to bark at her.

"This is 'cause of you, right? 'Cause you're a miserable shit lawyer!"

Miss Thompson took a deep breath.

"I saw your mother in the courtroom," she said, in an even tone. "I gave her the news, and she was very upset. I tried my best to calm her down and let her know I have a handle on it—that you'll be home soon."

But I wouldn't cut her an inch of slack, and stared her down.

Miss Thompson stood up and started stuffing papers into her briefcase.

"Oh, yeah, and thanks for all those times you never picked up the phone or called my mother back!"

"I don't like the system much either, Martin. The truth is, you get what you pay for," she popped off. "The city picks up this bill. I represent over fifty clients like you at the same time, *all* brothers or Hispanics. It's delicatessen-style justice in here. Take a number and wait. That's how it works."

Then Miss Thompson walked out the door and the CO came back inside to get me.

CHAPTER

By the time I got back to the pen, it had cooled way down. Still, the dudes who were being sent back to the Island weren't happy. And anyone who'd got off light wasn't going to smile too much over it. Not in there.

Sitting on one of the benches meant you'd have to move if somebody who was cranked up wanted your seat, or that you'd have to fight to keep it. I wasn't interested in any of that shit. So I stood up, hoping to get put on one of the next buses out.

A guy in a Nike sweatshirt was shadowboxing in the corner, trying to keep himself together. He was breathing hard and starting to really sweat. He'd rest with his hands wrapped tight around the bars, like they were around somebody's throat. Then he'd start up again to fight another round.

Those two kids who were ready to mix it up before stood

at opposite ends of the pen now. But I sensed that any little spark in between could set things off again.

Within a few minutes the COs called out close to twenty of us, and I got shackled to the one who wanted to take on that whole crew by himself.

We were among the last pairs onto the bus and were sitting close to the front. He spent half the trip glaring back at two kids from that crew who were shackled together.

Some big dude right behind us was pissed off. He kept cursing about how his own boys did him dirty in court, testifying against him.

"I'll kill all those bastards, and the DA. I'll blaze somebody right here, too. Don't think I won't," he warned, with his voice starting to crack.

You've got to watch your back when somebody gets desperate and blind mad like that. The CO was all over that dude, and I thought he might even lock him up in the cage.

"I'll put my foot up your ass if you don't stop!" screamed the CO. "Now shut up!"

"Fuck everybody!" the dude said.

While the CO was busy with him, my partner mouthed something to his fan club in the back. And I saw them steaming over what he said.

The bus passed through the first checkpoint and started over the bridge to Rikers. The sun pushed through the windows and struck me dead square in the face. It was shining off the bay, too. And I tried to pretend that I was heading to Rockaway Beach instead of jail. I even remembered a day as a little kid when Pops took me fishing there and caught a horseshoe crab by the tail with his bare hands. Only that memory got bounced from my brain by the first good bump we hit.

That damn bridge always seems longer when you're going back. But you'd rather have it go on forever than drop you off on Rikers Island.

Getting off the bus, that big dude broke down bawling. I guess from the stress. The CO must have taken him for a real herb, because he slapped him in the head as we were walking across the yard and said, "Shut up, crybaby!"

But that dude turned man again in a hurry. He tackled the CO on the spot, dragging the inmate he was chained to with him.

The other officers in the receiving yard ran over to help. That's when those kids from the back saw their chance.

They came at my partner, and I got caught in the middle. I'd been through enough that day and was ready to fight. But it was nearly impossible being chained to somebody. It was like two sets of Siamese twins trying to beat on each other, only that other pair was working with the same brain.

Before I got hit, I saw the spiderweb tattoo on one of their necks and the light reflecting off the burner in his hand. I threw my arms up, swinging back as hard as I could. Then I felt the side of my face get warm, and I tried to touch it with my cuffed hands.

The two of them jumped back into the crowd of inmates. I tried to go after them, but I got pushed down by COs.

I could feel the blood between my cheek and the ground.

That tattooed kid had cut me across the face with a razor.

The sharp sting started to pulse high on my cheek. Then it went racing down my entire body, like I'd been sliced from head to toe. Suddenly, I was paralyzed with fear, and I was too shook to even cry.

CHAPTER 5

Inside the clinic, COs were taking Polaroids of my face and asking me for a statement. Only I was in too much pain to even think about talking.

Then a doctor came at me wearing a mask and gloves, saying, "You'll barely feel this." When I woke up from that needle he gave me, the right side of my face was totally numb. And in the metal frame of the bed next to mine, I could see the bandages taped from the top of my skull to the bottom of my jaw.

I couldn't keep track of all the fears running through my brain—about what I was going to look like, how nasty a scar I would have, if the cut would ever heal. I kept closing my eyes, hoping everything would go away. But it was just blood-soaked bandages, white curtains, and inmates handcuffed to beds every time I opened them again.

I'd seen bad stitching on inmates before. That's because doctors on Rikers are usually just starting out, or couldn't keep a good job in a hospital. So they come to work in jail where nobody can fire them.

I'd heard lots of kids talk about getting their stitches fixed up right out in the world. They say how they're going to sue the doctor, or the jail for letting them get cut. Now there I was, seventeen years old, and I wasn't sure if my face was going to look like a jigsaw puzzle. I just knew I didn't want to see any more than I could in the frame of that bed.

An officer wearing a blue Windbreaker and holding a clipboard stepped to me. He closed the curtains behind him, like the dudes in the other beds wouldn't be able to hear us after that. He was wearing street clothes, and if it wasn't for the badge hooked to his belt, I could have sworn he was a social worker.

"How you feelin', Martin?" he asked, reading my name off a medical chart.

I didn't have an answer for him.

"It's criminal what somebody did to you," he said. "What are you gonna do to set this right?"

It didn't take him long to get into his rap. He was with the squad that tracks gangs through the jails, and his favorite saying was, "Just tell." No matter what was wrong, it could get fixed easy. "Just tell."

"Never mind *you*," he went on. "Some gangbanger put your mother through even worse pain. You're a minor, so we had to call and tell her what happened. You *know* she was upset. She probably won't get any sleep tonight because of what some punk did. Don't let him do your mother like that," he said. "Just tell."

There was nothing to say. Snitching on that kid wasn't good enough. I wanted to cut him back. I wanted to run up and slice him across the face like he'd done to me. I wouldn't care how much time I got for it.

Anyway, that CO didn't really care.

He was just like the ones who were supposed to search that kid who'd cut me before he got back onto the bus at the courthouse. They were all just going through the motions to pick up a paycheck.

The COs in the yard should have seen the kid who cut me. They didn't need to play me for a snitch.

Inmates on Rikers Island have a code: snitches get stitches.

I already had the stitches. I didn't need to be a pawn in anybody's game.

WEDNESDAY, JUNE 3

CHAPTER

By the next day, all that medication wore off, and the right side of my face was screaming. It hurt so bad I wanted to rip that metal railing off the side of the bed and go running down the corridor with it cuffed to my wrist, sparking on the floor behind me. I wanted to run through the front gate, across that damn bridge, and all the way home until the pain stopped.

Kids on Rikers are always trying to get sent to the clinic for medication. Most inmates will do anything to get high and kill time. The COs in the housing units can give out Tylenol, and lots of kids build up a supply. Then they take them all at once to get a buzz. Some dudes will even smoke ground-up orange peels, like weed, to get high. They'll dry the peels in the sun, on a window ledge. Then they'll roll up a fat "Sunkist blunt" with pages torn out from the Holy Bible.

But I didn't want any part of feeling good on Rikers Island. For five months I'd just wanted out of jail, and now I wanted out of the clinic.

The COs put the phones out that night.

One of the officers unhooked me from the bed and said, "You should call your family. Let them know you're okay."

He was right. But I didn't know what I was going to say to them.

I practiced in my head for maybe ten minutes and kept changing it every time. I needed to sound like I could handle it. That getting cut was no big deal. Only I couldn't lay out the words the way I wanted. So I finally just held my breath and dialed.

"I was just thinking about you, child," said Grandma.

I knew right away from the sound of her voice that Mom hadn't told her what happened. And I wasn't going to either.

"I was thinking 'bout you, too, Grandma. 'Bout how much I miss *you*, even more than your cooking," I said.

"I'll make your favorite, stew, to celebrate when you get home," she said.

"I can almost taste it now," I told her.

Then Mom got on the phone and I could almost feel her standing next to me. My little sisters were calling out my name in the background when she asked low, "How bad is it?"

"Not any worse than the cuts I got when I was a kid, except it's on my face," I answered. "Nothing to stress over."

But she wasn't having any of that.

"I'd have been there today if I coulda got off from work at Key Food without getting fired. But I couldn't. So it'll have to be Saturday," Mom said. "I love you, Martin. I pray for you to come home every night. Just don't do anything stupid to get even with nobody. They'll keep you locked up longer. You hear?"

"I love you, too, Mom. See you Saturday," I answered, taking the phone away from the left side of my face.

Then I thought about that tattooed kid who'd cut me. I could see every hook and line in that spiderweb inked onto his neck. And I wondered how he'd ever got so close to my family, all the way from Rikers Island.

Later on, I got discharged from the clinic and found out they were changing my housing unit. Maybe they were screwing with me for not snitching or figured that after five months in the same place, I knew enough people to put a price on that kid's head. But whatever the reason, I was getting moved.

It was after nine o'clock when they brought me back to Mod-3 to pack up. Almost everyone was watching TV inside the dayroom, except for a few kids already asleep in their beds. No one from the house had been on the bus back to Rikers with me, so none of them knew what happened. They probably all thought I got released from court. Only there I was, walking into the house with bandages across my right cheek, about to pack all my shit into a plastic laundry bag.

The COs wouldn't let anyone out of the dayroom. They're always worried that somebody will see you moving as their last chance to settle a score. But I didn't have any real enemies, and I could see dudes pressed up against the big windows as I went through my bucket. They were pointing to their faces and looking at me, cutting themselves with a finger to see how it might feel.

I knew some of them were watching to make sure that I only took stuff out of my own bucket. More than one guy had become a sneak thief while the rest of the house was bottled up somewhere.

When I'd finished packing, I tied the plastic bag up in my blanket and threw it on top of my mattress. Then I pulled the mattress to the floor and started dragging it all behind me, like I'd seen other kids do when they moved out.

Up at the Plexiglas bubble, one of the regular house COs gave my card over to an escort officer. I could see my picture stapled to the corner. Only it looked like a picture of somebody else now, somebody without stitches.

I didn't know where I was going and I wouldn't ask.

The escort officer led me out of Mod-3, and I headed down the main corridor, homeless.

At the end of the corridor there was a woman CO at a desk next to an iron door. She looked old and tired, like a grandmother sitting behind a kitchen table.

She stared at the bandages on my face and said, "Honey, why would you let that kind of trouble find you?"

I dropped my eyes to the floor.

She groaned as she got up, and I heard her turn one of the big metal keys on her ring in the door.

Mom would warn me all the time about getting into trouble. Whenever I went out at night she'd tell me to stay home. Sometimes she'd almost beg me. But I *was* at home, sitting alone on the stoop outside my building, when I got arrested.

This muscle-bound dude stepped to me, and I tried to front, acting tough. I was breathing easy when he only wanted to know where to cop some weed. I told him about the spot up the avenue and even felt good about it when he called me, *"my man."*

That undercover cop scored what he wanted, because a police cruiser rolled up my block about five minutes later. I almost couldn't believe those cops were looking for me. But they weren't fucking around.

Mom saw the flashing lights through our living-room window.

She stuck her head out and yelled, "Martin, get your ass upstairs now!"

That's when she saw them cuffing me. By the time she got outside, I was already in the squad car. The cops told her I was being charged with steering. She had no idea what that meant.

I remember her screaming at them, "My son didn't steal any car!"

If she wasn't crying so much, it might have even been funny.

CHAPTER

I stepped through the iron door and was surprised to suddenly be outside in the cool night air. The smell of the jail was gone. That funk that comes with the dirty laundry and rotting garbage was behind me now.

It was tight between the buildings of the jail, and the cement path was lined with a tall fence covered in razor wire. The path led out to an open yard I'd never seen before, beneath the clouds and stars. There were rows of lights shining high up on the tops of poles, two basketball courts laid out side by side, a handball wall, and some bleachers.

I felt like I was back home on the playground, and my mood just picked right up. It felt like I'd carried my mattress from my *real* house to camp out overnight in the park. And maybe those were even the same stars I used to wish on when I was a kid.

The officer told me to sit in the bleachers while he showed my paperwork to the CO on duty in the yard. I sat there looking up at the sky, wishing I could do my time on those bleachers. I would sit through the longest night that anyone could imagine. Then the sun would come up and I could go home.

And despite the pain I was in, it felt that sweet.

The yard was surrounded by six white bubbles, the kind people play tennis in during the winter. I never saw anyone walking around the jail with a tennis racket, so I figured that's where they keep the inmates in this part of the jail.

The bubbles sat together in pairs and had a big "N" or "S" painted on them. I knew from living in the main building that it meant the north and south side of each house. The sides were connected by a little station, and that was probably for the COs.

I knew I'd be starting all over again. I'd be walking into some strange house like a new jack, with a fresh cut on my face and a lot to prove. For another sixteen days, until I went back to court, I'd have to buckle down and keep it real.

The officer came back to the bleachers and said, "You've been assigned to Sprung #3, *my man*."

I put my hands up against the wall and Officer Johnson kicked both my ankles out hard. My feet were spread as far apart as they could go and still be standing. In front of us was a set of double doors that led to the officers' station in Sprung #3.

That's where I'd spent all of thirty seconds before Johnson brought me outside for a private introduction and to hear his house rules. Behind us was another set of double doors that led back out to the yard. We were in *his* private jail now, a ten-foot space where he made all the rules and kept them with his fists.

Johnson was big and black, and looked more like a grizzly bear than a CO.

"I'm here from four till midnight, five nights a week," he growled. "Do the wrong thing and I will personally shit on you. This is my house and you're only renting. I don't know what you did to deserve that cut. But try any of that nonsense out here and I'll ship your ass back to the building where they can take another piece of you."

He ended his speech by slapping me in the ribs with a huge open hand. When I caught my breath, I stood up and followed him back inside.

It was twenty after ten by then. It's always lights-out at ten o'clock. But most inmates lie awake in the dark for a good part of the night. This house was no different. They'd been stirring like mice since I walked through the front door. They were sizing me up, trying to figure out where I fit in their food chain.

I remembered how tough it was when I first got to Rikers, carving out a place for myself and trying not to become any-body's herb. I'd learned plenty in the past five months about how it all goes down, and I was hoping to get some space without having to fight for it. I had been in Mod-3 for so long, new jacks watched *me* to see how it would go.

Out here, I was going to have to do all the watching for a while.

CHAPTER

The count was low on the north side, and when the COs looked at my ID card they saw the number forty staring at them.

"Bed forty is open on the north," said one of Johnson's partners. "All we got to do with this kid's card is change Mod-3 to Sprung #3."

My world had been kicked upside down since yesterday, but on Rikers Island I was still going to be called "Forty."

My bed was in the back of the house, near the bathroom. I tossed my shit into the bucket, put my mattress on the frame, and got into bed. There was a CO watching our side from a desk up front. He spent most of the night reading a newspaper with his feet up, like nothing ever happens out here.

I wasn't convinced, and I stayed up for a few hours staring at the high ceiling. There were big fans that hung down from the top of the Sprung, and I watched the blades turning slow. I could feel the air moving all around me. And I kept the blanket away from my face so I could see anyone coming.

There was no Plexiglas bubble for the officers to hole up in, where the phone and emergency alarm were in case the entire house went zoo. Here, the officers' desk was right out in the open where kids could just rush it if they wanted. But the COs didn't seem uptight about it.

COs inside the jail don't carry guns; only the ones patrolling outside the gates do. If they had guns on the inside, inmates would forever be scheming on how to wrestle one away. But the COs inside aren't scared, because they stick up for each other. That uniform connects them like one big gang. Only they're more dangerous than any gang I know, because they have badges and the courts to back them up.

Inmates have the COs outnumbered, maybe thirty to one. But they're all apart, fighting over every little thing, and the COs are too much together. Even if some COs don't like each other, they hate inmates even worse.

The only time a CO has to worry is if a bunch of inmates jump him all at once. And every CO has a personal alarm clipped to his shirt. When he hits the button, a signal goes off in a control room up at the front of the jail. The riot squad comes running on the double. And those animals will hit anything that moves, including kids with their hands up in the air.

Two kids on the midnight suicide watch came through. I could see they were checking me out. One of them even flashed some fake-ass gang signs at me, but I looked right through him.

Midnight suicide is a good job for an inmate, but you got to have some juice to get it. The COs have to like you and think you're down with their program. Lots of times they'll give their enforcers the job as a reward for helping to keep the house in line. Other times the house snitch will be on midnights. But they're usually all down with Five-O in some way.

The kids on midnight get to stay up all night and sleep most of the day. Besides the fifty-cents-a-night pay, you get $150 put into your account if you stop an inmate from trying to kill himself. In Mod-3, we used to talk about having a fake suicide so we could all split the money. But no one ever wanted to get turned in and have to go to Bellevue Hospital for observation in the mental ward.

"Yo, Forty," whispered some kid from the next row of beds. "We need a new Maytag in the house. Wash all our clothes in the bathroom sink, and we'll let you live around here."

That kid didn't know a thing about how I carried myself around a house. He was just going by the first thing he saw— that somebody had sliced me like a Thanksgiving turkey.

I heard a couple of them laugh when I called for the officer.

They probably thought I was looking for protection. But I said in a voice loud enough for the whole north side to hear, "CO, I need to use the bathroom."

The laughing stopped.

I was calling out anyone who wanted to follow me inside. I wanted to see the layout of the bathroom, too, before morning, when it would be full of kids. Then I couldn't get jumped so easy.

The bathroom is the best place for inmates to fight, away from the eyes of the COs. During the day, kids watch the door and let you know when the COs are coming. I walked through the open doorway and looked it over. It was bigger than most, maybe fifteen feet wide and fifty feet long. None of the stalls had doors, and the showers were way at the end and up a few steps. You could have a real war in a cave like this, and the COs up at the front of the house would never know.

There was a row of polished metal mirrors over the sinks. All mirrors on Rikers are made of metal. They don't allow glass in jail. It's too easy to smash and break into a thousand weapons. You could use a match to burn a sliver of glass into the end of a toothbrush, and it would be just as good as a razor.

I looked at myself in one of the mirrors. And if I could, I would have ripped it straight off—not only because of the bandages on my face, or the pain I was in, but the way I looked older after all the time I'd shitted away.

Then I leaned up against a stall and waited to see if anyone would show.

Less than a minute later, a skinny kid walked inside. His name, "Jersey," was barely out of his mouth when I stepped to him. Jersey wasn't a fighter, just a kid they could amp up into trying me.

I tackled his ass, pinning him to the floor. He couldn't have been more than sixteen. I had a year and at least twenty pounds on him. My eyes were locked onto his, and he was staring up at my face. We stayed like that without saying a word until I yanked him up by the front of his shirt.

"Stay right here till one of your crew comes and gets you," I said, sitting him down on a toilet seat. "Tell your boss I'm a peaceful dude. But I'm not gonna be pushed around."

The sweat was rolling down his face as he nodded his head. And when I knew I could turn my back on him, I went over to one of the urinals and took a piss.

I left the bathroom and coughed a couple of times just to let everyone know I was the one still standing. Then I spit into the garbage pail and got back into bed.

Another kid went inside to find out what had happened to Jersey. I could see by his shadow that he was big and slow. He wasn't the boss, just another "doldier," a combination doer and soldier. Then the kid came back outside, with Jersey walking even slower behind him.

After that, I tried to catch some sleep a little bit at a time.

THURSDAY,
JUNE 4

CHAPTER
9

The sun came up and the whole north side went from dark to light. There are no window shades or curtains in jail, so anyone wanting to sleep past daybreak had to bury his head beneath a blanket or pillow.

I sat up in the light and looked around to see if anyone was still interested in me. There were only a handful of kids awake, and none of them wanted to even trade looks. Jersey had given his crew the lowdown by now. And anyone that hadn't heard yet could tell by my face that I had a history.

Inmates get cuts on their faces for different reasons. You might get in deep juggling and decide not to pay. Sometimes a crew gets a real stranglehold on a house and you're down with another outfit. Maybe you're a herb that somebody used to prop himself up, or you're a snitch and somebody was getting even. I didn't fit into any of that. But people were going to try and place me somewhere. That's just how it is in jail. Every-body has a place, and nobody wants you to fuck up the order, especially if it puts you on top of them.

"Breakfast," a CO called as low as he could.

Only two kids got up to eat.

The COs call breakfast real early, when almost everybody is still asleep. This way they don't have to hassle with getting half a house back and forth to the mess hall. They never have it easier than when everyone is sleeping, so they try to keep it like that as long as possible. That means most inmates are thinking about lunch from the moment they wake up. I usually bought stuff for the morning during weekly commissary, like cookies and soda, using the money Mom put into my account. But there were no snacks in my bucket now.

Most dudes spend their account money on cigarettes and live off jail food. But I'd rather have a settled stomach than a smoke any day. Besides, there's always a cloud of smoke hanging over the dayroom that you can suck in for free. Dudes who don't even smoke buy cigarettes because they're easy to juggle and you can get almost anything for them. And the jail will sell you cigarettes in commissary even if you're under eighteen. If kids didn't smoke, they'd be wired all day and there would be nothing but fights.

I saw in the newspaper that some kid in Texas sued the jail out there after he got cancer. He was only seventeen, but they sold him stoves anyway. They had to pay him millions because he saved all his commissary receipts and could prove it.

Dudes are always talking about suing the jail. But for all the times the COs beat our asses without a reason, they get bagged for selling cigarettes to a minor. I guess that's the way this fucked-up justice system works.

Nearly two hours later, a CO hollered at the top of his lungs, "Let's go, *ladies*! Rise and shine!"

I was shocked. It was just before eight o'clock and the COs were serious about getting the whole house up.

"I warned you yesterday about moving your lazy ass!" yelled a CO, before flipping the bed over on a kid who didn't get up fast enough.

Now I knew there was some kind of schedule to keep.

Most kids were still walking around in a daze. They were either heading for the bathroom or taking down their washed clothes, which were drying on the air vents.

I made my bed, waiting for the count.

The entire north side of Sprung #3 could see my face now, and kids were starting to say shit as they passed.

Dude must be havin' his period on his cheek.

That's why all the Tampax.

He got done up like cold cuts at the deli.

Other kids just shook their heads because they knew it could happen to them, too.

The CO blew a whistle and everybody stood by their beds, counting off. Most of the voices were tired and weak, fading into the high, round ceiling of that tennis bubble. But I could tell right away which dudes were part of the main crew. They knew I was listening and wanted to count off like they were somebody.

"Twenty-seven!" boomed the voice of the dude who'd said I was going to Maytag for them. He was short and squat, but his muscles were really chiseled. And he sounded like he stood, cocked and ready to go.

I waited my turn and loudly said, "Forty!"

After the COs told us to deuce it up, we marched out of Sprung #3 and into the yard, with the south side following behind.

I saw the back end of Sprung #2 disappearing into one of the trailers. Sprung #1 was at the gate of their house, waiting for us to pass, and a captain in a sharp white shirt was eyeballing it all.

The COs took us across the basketball courts, and then we stopped in front of another trailer. One of the kids at the head of the line had the box with all of our ID cards, and one of the COs was carrying the logbook. So I knew we'd be out of the house for a while.

A civilian walked past with a yellow ID card clipped to his shirt.

One of our dudes called to him, "Yo, mister, pick me for the GED."

That's when it hit me. We were going to school.

Out in the world, I'd finished my junior year at Jamaica High School in December, right before I got locked up, even though it took me an extra semester to get there. I'd held a

70 average, and had even passed the English statewide exam a year early. But now here I was, walking into some beat-up school trailer on Rikers Island with almost a hundred other inmates.

My old house had a GED teacher that came by a couple of times a week. But I wanted to graduate from high school for real, and I always thought I was just about to go home. So I never bothered with it. But Sprung #3 was a legit schoolhouse five days a week.

There was an olive-skinned teacher with tight, curly hair just inside the door of the trailer, sitting on top of a table like he was in his living room. He was calling inmates by their first names as we walked in, making a real show of how many he knew.

"Michael, Dontel, Julio, Rodney," he said, without missing a beat. "I got Sprung #3 names on lockdown."

Some dudes slapped his hand as they passed and said, "Demarco, the best."

I heard him call out "New jack, don't know you yet" to kids before and after me. But he looked *me* square in the face without the comedy and said, "My name's Demarco. Good to meet you."

The whole house was deuced up in the middle of the hall when a CO screamed, "Cockroaches disappear!"

Kids scrambled for their classes, but us new jacks were still standing there. One of the COs was holding open a door and pointing inside.

"In here for today," he snapped. "The next placement test is tomorrow. Just stay quiet, and whatever you do, don't fuck up."

It was a storeroom where they kept extra tables and lockers. There were seven of us standing against the wall. We spread out as best we could, and for a while nobody talked or even moved much. Then one of the kids put two tables together for a bed and stretched himself out on top. Somebody else started trying all the lockers. One of them even popped open, but it was only filled with schoolbooks.

There was a tall, wiry white dude with us, and from what I saw he was the only one in the house. Just a few of them had passed through Mod-3 in all the time I was there. White dudes are usually real quiet in jail and keep to themselves, because they've got no power and nobody to watch their backs.

He was sitting on the floor when one of the kids asked, "How the fuck did you ever get locked up? Didn't you tell that blind judge you were a cracker?"

It got tense for a second, but the white dude looked that kid right in the eye and answered, "I didn't know I was a cracker. Am I a Ritz or a saltine?"

The kid who was trying to sleep on the tables laughed so hard he almost rolled off. And after that slick comeback, everybody there gave that white dude a free pass.

I liked the way he handled himself and decided to call him Ritz, because it rolled easier off the tongue.

CHAPTER 10

After a while, a small white officer with a pinched face came inside and pulled a chair to the middle of the room. He took a store-bought ham and Swiss cheese sandwich out of a paper bag and started to unwrap it. Our eyes were glued to that sandwich like he was taking the clothes off a beautiful woman.

"For all of you losers who can't read, my name is *Mister* or *Officer* Carter," he said, pointing to the nameplate beneath his badge.

He took a big bite out of the sandwich. Then he reached into his pocket and pulled out a wad of bills. Carter wiped the corners of his mouth with the cash and said, "I guess you guys haven't seen any dead presidents lately."

"Can I just touch one?" somebody asked.

"Sure, kid, it's probably what got you here," he answered.

"Mr. Carter, why are you torturing us like this?" asked the kid fingering the bills.

"Because you're inmates, sweetheart. And as long as you keep praying to this green god, you'll be coming back to jail and I can support my family. I just feel sorry for your mothers, that's all," answered Carter.

A teacher with little glasses hanging off the tip of his crooked nose came in and walked right past us to his locker. It was like we were all invisible or maybe he was some kind of robot.

"Mr. Murray," said Carter, still waving his bundle around. "Teach these guys about supply and demand in your class, will ya?"

"I teach history, not economics," he said. "But if you boys don't walk a straight line in my room, I'll put you out in the hall with Carter and you can hold up the wall all day."

"That's right. Fuck up in school and your asses are mine," warned Carter.

On his way back out, Mr. Murray stopped at the door. His four eyes settled on a kid in the corner and he grinned wide.

"Didn't this one get placed in a class last week?" he asked, pointing him out.

Carter grabbed the kid by his ear and twisted hard.

"Back to class, asswipe," snarled Carter.

He took his sandwich in one hand and dragged the kid out of the room with the other, kicking him in the behind as they went.

Then Murray looked at us with a fucked-up smile and said, "You boys never learn, do you?"

CHAPTER
11

A minute later, that kid with the chiseled muscles bounced into the room like he owned it.

He looked us up and down and a couple of the kids even took a step backward. I was sitting on the floor, leaning up against the wall, so I didn't move.

"The name's Cedric, but everybody calls me Brick," he said, flexing a forearm. "That's 'cause I fall down hard on people."

Brick probably wasn't any stronger than a lot of kids with a decent build. He just looked harder, and had his thug act wrapped supertight.

I kept my eyes on him as he talked. And once it looked like he had everybody else in that room backed down, he began to bark at me.

"Don't listen to what the COs tell you. *I* run this house. You want to use the phone during prime time? You need a loan till commissary comes? That's all *me*," he bragged.

I'd seen kids like him before. He was a straight-up gang-ster in what was looking more and more like a soft house.

"I heard what you did to Jersey," said Brick. "I don't hold it against you. I could use a real fighter on my payroll. We'll talk later. Okay?"

But I played him cold and stiff and didn't say a word.

That's when Brick turned to the other kids and said, "Maybe they cut his tongue out, too."

They all laughed with him, except for Ritz. I guess he'd got used to standing alone on Rikers.

Most kids understand what a thug like Brick can do. They don't want to get caught on the wrong side of him. So they usually play it safe, going along with whatever he says.

"I'll check you chumps later," Brick said, bouncing back out.

About an hour after that, the COs called the house out for lunch.

The mess hall workers were mostly kids from our Sprung. Brick and his crew had spots at the front of the mess hall line, while I was almost at the rear. I could see from the mountain of food on their plates that they carried a lot of weight in the house. We had franks and beans all mixed together, with white bread on the side.

It hurt like anything to eat with those stitches. And even though I'd shoveled everything into the left side of my mouth, the right side moved along whenever I chewed.

I finished what they gave me and was still hungry. But

none of the mess hall workers would serve me seconds when I went back.

"Who you?" one of them asked.

"Nobody," another one answered.

And I had to stomach watching Brick and his crew toss their trays in the trash, still half full of food.

CHAPTER

12

After lunch, the COs put me and the other new jacks back
inside that storeroom. I had just settled into a comfort-
able spot when a voice from the hall hollered, "Forty,
you got a visit."

I'd been trying not to think about it, but deep down I knew
Mom couldn't wait till Saturday. Having her see me like this was
going to be hard. And I felt worse for her than I did for myself.

All the anger and frustration flamed up inside of me fast,
like a fever. I wanted to scream out loud.

Fuck that kid for slicing my face!

Fuck him for putting my mother through this shit!

And fuck me for getting my black ass locked up!

I couldn't get a handle on it until I hit the yard and felt the
sun and wind on my face.

An officer escorted me into the main building, past my old
house, and up to the visit floor.

The COs there took my clothes and gave me an orange jumpsuit and slippers to match. That outfit labeled me an inmate and made it impossible to sneak out with the visitors. And that bandaged cut on my face marked me the same way.

The open visit floor is always packed with women. Mothers and grandmothers usually wear their church clothes. Wives and girlfriends always dress sexy. Sometimes a guy will pay more attention to another dude's girl than to his own family. Inmates have even got into fights right there over looking at somebody else's shorty.

Women and kids are the only ones who can handle the hassle of coming to see you. Most men would start a riot over the crap they get put through. It's that crazy.

First, visitors get a long speech from the captain about smuggling in drugs and razors. There's even a box where visitors can dump the contraband they brought without getting arrested. Then the COs search everybody for real. If they find anything on you they'll lock your ass up, too.

It could all take a couple of hours. Then your visitors only get to see you for a lousy fifteen minutes.

Forget about your homeboys. They mostly cut you loose when you're locked down. Mine did. My two best friends from my block, dudes I grew up with, hadn't visited once. I don't even mention their names to Mom anymore. It's like they don't exist to me now. Only people that *really* care about you, like your close family, would go through that kind of trouble just to see you.

CHAPTER
13

She was sitting at a green plastic table.

Her eyes followed me all the way across the floor until the CO let me go. Then Mom jumped up and hugged me tight without letting her head brush against my bandages. She held me like that till we could both keep from crying.

"You're still my baby, Martin," Mom said, stroking the side of my face that was still whole.

I looked into her sad eyes and thought about everything I ever did wrong to put us there. Then we sat down right in the middle of Rikers Island and were a family.

She told me about my sisters' good report cards from grade school. She said that both Trisha and Tina had parts in the school play, and that Grandma's asthma was getting worse.

"Maybe there's one good thing coming out of this," I said, trying to ease her worries. "I'm starting up high school in a new house. I got more than two weeks left here. Maybe I can take some kind of test to get some credits toward senior year."

"Thank you for giving him the strength," she said, looking up to heaven. "Lord, thank you for his mind."

Pops hadn't been home in seven years after he caught a second charge in prison for nearly killing somebody in a fight. I knew Mom was afraid that would happen to me.

"I can see the hatred in your eyes," she said. "Don't let it burn."

"It's all right," I told her.

"I don't want to hear nothin' about some damn *man's code*," Mom warned me. "Forget about getting even. I've been on too many of these visits in my life. I'm tired of coming to jail. Please, Martin. Let it go. I swear I got enough anger inside of me for this whole family."

My sisters made a drawing for me. There was a sun in bright yellow crayon and all of us standing in front of our apartment building except for Pops. He'd got buried so deep in the system that my sisters didn't even remember him living with us. And since I'd been locked up on Rikers, Mom stopped visiting him upstate so she could see *me* on Saturdays.

I asked how she'd got off work from Key Food and she answered, "You never mind that. I do what I have to do for my children."

Mom wanted to see my face under the bandages, but I said no.

"I haven't even looked yet," I said. "I'm gonna wait till it's healed more."

Then she kissed me on the forehead one time. Mom said

she still hadn't told my sisters or Grandma what happened, and I was glad for that. I knew she wouldn't tell Pops because he'd get crazy mad over it, and he had enough problems to worry about already.

It's only on a visit that you want the time to go slow when you're in jail. After a few more minutes, the CO came back and told Mom it was time to leave.

CHAPTER
14

By the time I got back to the Sprungs, school was over and the whole house was in the yard for rec.

There aren't many times when the north and south sides of a house get mixed. It happens in the mess hall—only there the COs can eagle-eye you good at your table. In the Sprungs, it happened in school, too. But I could already see that some of those teachers, like Murray, probably had their noses in everybody's business.

When a house is at rec, lots of things between inmates get taken care of. That's because the jail has rec officers on patrol, and they don't really know you. They only care that kids don't throw down and fight. The regular COs stay back at the house with anyone who just wants to lie around. That gives inmates from different sides a chance to take care of business.

There were two games of hoops going on in the yard.

The egg-shaped basketball that kids were using on one court didn't have any grips left. There were bubbles pushing out of the seams, and it even bounced sideways sometimes. It was strictly welfare.

That was the game for the guys without any juice.

Ritz was playing there, and even with that piece-of-shit ball he was all right. I guess if a white dude wanted to get some respect on Rikers Island, passing the ball to somebody for an open layup is a good way to start.

Brick was standing on the sideline under the *right* basket, where dudes there were playing with the good ball.

He had a couple of oversized doldiers with him and was going over a list of what he was owed, right out in the open.

"Dude owes me six cigarettes and seven beef sticks," Brick said, pointing to his paper. "This one owes two whole packs of cookies. And this joker right here owes me a two-liter Pepsi."

Like any thug, Brick was smiling and laughing with kids. There's always good times as long as everybody knows their place and pays off.

I would have tried to get into one of the basketball games, but I was worried about my stitches. I didn't need to take an elbow to the face, by accident or any other way.

There were fifteen Spanish dudes living on the north side of our house, and they had control of the handball wall. That was their turf, and I wasn't looking to push my way around over there either. So I threw myself on the ground and started knocking out push-ups.

I started off by doing twenty-five, with my face beginning to throb. Then I took a short break. Halfway through the second set, my arms were trembling from the strain, and I needed to grit my teeth to make the last few, stretching the muscles in my cheek till I thought my stitches were going to bust wide open.

That night in the house, almost everybody was sitting in the dayroom watching TV. A kid called Shaky was squeezing the two ends of the antenna together so the picture would come in clear. He had to do it from behind the set or no one would be able to see. There wasn't a chair high enough for Shaky to sit down on and still reach the antenna. So he spent the night standing up and looking out at us from behind the set. And after a couple of hours of that, kids started flipping him cookies as pay.

I could tell straight off that Shaky wasn't right in the head.

During commercials, they would mute the sound and let Shaky tell stories about all the dudes he'd beat up.

"I cracked him with my *loco power*, and then karate-kicked him in the nuts. Bam!" Shaky said, nearly falling over from showing the kick.

Kids would poke holes in his story, and he'd start to shake all over, getting nervous.

"It's true," pleaded Shaky, kissing two fingers on his right hand and touching them to his heart. "Word to mother. All true."

Sometimes when a kid is *off* like that he gets adopted by

the house. They use him for a clown and try to take care of him. And I could tell that's what was happening with Shaky.

I spent half the night watching TV and half watching the three inmate phones by the officers' desk. The COs ran slot time from six o'clock to seven thirty. That's when everybody in the house gets five minutes on the phone. It's also when a lot of herbs get ripped off for their pin numbers. Another inmate can surf over your shoulder and pick up your code. Then he'll be dialing on your account for free until it's empty.

Seven thirty to nine o'clock was prime time, and you had to have some juice to dial. That's when a doldier from Brick's crew was always hanging around the phones, collecting from kids who wanted to make another call. His boys took turns on and off, and I got to see his whole posse on the north side.

Barnett was a big black dude. He looked kind of soft, but he was too big to fight without a good reason. Luis was smaller and more solid-looking. He dealt with most of the Spanish dudes for Brick. Then there was Jersey. I didn't expect that Brick would send him my way again.

In all the time I watched, not a single kid challenged the system. And I wondered if Brick had it locked down like that on the south side, too.

FRIDAY, JUNE 5

CHAPTER 15

After we got to the school trailer the next morning, an assistant teacher rounded up the new jacks from all three Sprungs and brought us over to the mess hall to take a placement test.

He handed out the test facedown and then gave each of us a fresh sharpened, full-size PROPERTY OF DEPARTMENT OF EDU-CATION pencil.

"We collect every one of these," he fussed, waving a pencil. "If even one disappears, we'll have the officers search you all. Understand? We're not here to supply you with weapons."

"Now don't be giving these kids any bad ideas," snapped Ms. Armstrong, the CO with us. "They've already got too much nonsense on their minds."

I almost couldn't believe what I was holding. I touched the lead point with one of my fingertips. It was so long and sharp, you could stab someone clean through.

The dude sitting to my right had a tattoo of a cross on his neck. In my mind, I imagined it was that spiderweb on the kid who'd cut me. And for a few seconds, I gripped that pencil tight inside my fist, till that wave of anger passed.

House COs only give out pencils about the size of your thumb for writing letters. Even the pens you buy in commissary come without a hard, plastic cover. They just sell you the metal point and the tube filled with ink. So if you tried to stick someone with that, it would bend before it ever broke skin.

Ms. Armstrong was a combination CO and housemother. Inmates want this kind of women officer because when something breaks down, like the hot water, you can put it in their ear that it's not right. They're usually real sensitive about kids being locked up and not getting services. They'll keep dialing the phone till somebody comes out and fixes what's wrong.

She was black, with a round face and big hips. Most kids had a mother or aunt who looked and acted just like her.

"I got a son in junior high right now," said Ms. Armstrong, reading the test over our shoulders. "I help him with his homework all the time."

"He ever been locked up?" a kid asked.

"I didn't say I busted his ass, did I?" she came back.

Then Ms. Armstrong caught somebody just filling in the blanks without even looking at the questions.

"You want people to think you're stupid, boy?" she said, slapping him on the back of the head.

Halfway through, Demarco walked in and told us to put

our pencils down. The assistant giving the test got all nervous about it and went to the door to watch for who might be coming. I guess he didn't want to get in trouble for letting Demarco interrupt us.

"Look, even the teachers got to watch the door in jail," cracked Ms. Armstrong. "Only it's not the COs they're fearful of; it's the principal."

"I'm Demarco Costa," he said. "But what's really important is who all of you are. So let me hear your names."

Then Demarco pointed to us one by one, and kids said their names.

When Ritz said his new tag, everyone from that Sprung #3 storeroom broke up laughing.

Demarco looked at him funny and said, "Is Ritz your *last* name?"

"No, somebody called me a cracker. Then dudes decided I would be a Ritz because of my obvious style," he explained, with Demarco grinning from ear to ear. "But my real name is Walter."

When it was my turn, I said, "Forty."

"I might as well call you *table* or *chair*," Demarco said. "I'm not interested in knowing you like that."

I didn't know what to say back.

Then the next kid took his turn and it continued down the line.

I felt like I'd missed out on something good.

Demarco said that the test wasn't all a waste of time, and

that if we wanted to get put in the right class level or try for a GED, we should take it for real.

"I know it's not easy to think about school when you're locked up," he said. "But you want to show people, like a judge, that you're serious about what you do. And you don't want to fall behind everybody your age to get things, like a good job to support yourself and your family."

After hearing that, lots of kids were looking at Demarco like he was too good to be true for this place.

Demarco wasn't white, but he wasn't dark enough to be black either. Kids asked him what he was and he answered, "I'm a teacher."

The assistant started flapping his arms, like a bird that's about to take off, and came running back from the door. We picked our pencils up and everyone got quiet.

Demarco was looking up at the ceiling when a thin, middle-aged black woman in high heels and a dress that hung down to just above her bony knees walked into the mess hall and said, "Good morning, Mr. Costa."

She looked us up and down and said, "I'm Ms. Jackson, the principal here. Let's go over a few basic rules. When you're in class, you are to be respectful of"—*blah . . . blah . . . blah.*

I wanted to tell Demarco my name was Martin. But he moved behind the principal while she was talking, giving us all a thumbs-up before he slipped out the door.

CHAPTER
16

When school finished that day the COs took us shopping. A house never gets more excited than when it's going to commissary. Everybody has a list of what they want to buy, and it almost feels like Christmas.

We deuced it up and marched across the yard into the main building. The COs who work the corridor stopped us at the first gate.

The main corridor is maybe two city blocks long, with iron gates every hundred feet or so. This way if something big ever jumps off, the COs in the control booth can close the different gates with an electric switch and keep the fighting pinned down to just one area.

We were waiting because there was traffic up ahead. The corridor is like a highway. There's a line running down the center and you always walk on the right side, no matter which way you're headed.

Even though it happens, COs never want two houses to pass each other in the hall. Even when you're marching right up against the wall, there's only four or five feet between you and the dudes on the other side. If the two houses had bad blood and wanted to fight, there'd be no stopping it. The COs playing the centerline would get caught in the middle, and most inmates would enjoy that.

Sprung #2 was on its way back from shopping. They were all smiles, holding big paper bags filled with commissary.

"We bought all the food there was," said one of their kids. "Nothing left for you Sprung-bunnies. Sold out."

But everybody knew better than to take him serious.

One of the kids coming back must have just transferred over from Sprung #3. He held his bag up high and dropped his head behind it. Only some of our dudes recognized him and began blasting his name.

Harris!

It's that deadbeat Harris!

Brick tried to put the bite on him for whatever he owed right there.

"Pay up now, sucka," he snapped.

The kid got all shook. But Officer Carter wouldn't have any of that crap in the corridor.

House COs can get real tight in the halls and don't want to be shown up by their inmates in front of other officers standing post.

"Let me hear one more word and I'll turn this house back around!" barked Carter. "Do not disrespect me!"

For now, Brick backed off.

But I didn't take him for the kind that turned the other cheek.

We got to commissary, and I filled out an order sheet. I had only three bucks in my account. Mom filled it for me when she had a few extra dollars. I got a handful of beef sticks with it. They fit into my pocket, and nobody except the kid behind me knew what I'd bought.

I never liked beef sticks much until I got locked up. You can heat them over a match and it's like having a hot meal anytime you want.

Brick carried two big bags in each arm back to the Sprungs. I watched him unload his commissary while his goons made collections. He had so much shit to put away that he had to rent a bucket from another kid.

Barnett and Luis were walking around with a list of what kids owed. They even checked the receipts of what kids bought, just to make sure that no one was holding out on them.

Kids go to somebody like Brick to juggle because they don't have any money in their account.

It's usually two for one on the straight juggle, paying back twice what you borrowed. But if a shark like Brick has something dudes are really desperate for, or the house gets burned from commissary and nobody can shop, he can get even more.

That night, Barnett and Luis lumped up some kid in the bathroom. They beat him with wooden scrub brushes, swinging them over their heads inside of sweat socks so that the force coming down would be even harder. The kid was the cousin of Harris, the dude from Sprung #2 who'd beat Brick out of commissary. It was a lesson for anybody that wanted to get too slick.

Sometimes a herb gets lumped and doesn't tell the COs. But those goons hurt him so bad that he was bleeding and it wouldn't stop. The COs had to fill out reports and send him to the clinic.

Before the kid left, Johnson, that grizzly bear of a CO, made the whole house stand by their beds, like in a lineup.

"Everybody, on the double," roared Johnson. "Let's see who looks guilty."

The kid was scared shitless and wouldn't pick them out.

Johnson was pissed and cursed his ass for twenty minutes until the escort came to get him.

"We can't help you. Not if you stand there silent like a fucking mute," Johnson yelled. "It won't be on my conscience. No. When you don't speak up for yourself, it's all on you!"

When that kid got back from the clinic, the COs packed him up to another house for his own good.

SATURDAY, JUNE 6

CHAPTER
17

There was no school on the weekend, so the COs just let us sleep late. A guy named Sanchez had the bed next to mine. At eight o'clock we were the only ones awake on the north side and started to talk.

"My smart-mouthed lawyer told me to look at my watch," Sanchez said. "It was 4:57. He says, 'Three to five. That's how much time you're gonna cop out to on this drug charge.'"

Sanchez told me he had turned eighteen the week before. He'd been sitting in the Sprungs for nearly seven months, and even got his GED there.

He flashed a big grin as he reached into his school folder to show me the official diploma. And Sanchez was only still in class because he wanted to be, and because the teachers thought he was a good influence.

Then he talked about going upstate to do his three-year

bid, and the time he'd served so far on Rikers. That's when his face got real serious and the mustache over his lip started to twitch.

Maybe it was the bandages on my face that made him feel like I'd be as scared as he was.

"Upstate's going to be a nightmare. I've never even had to live in the main building on Rikers," he admitted, folding his arms across his chest. "It's been all Sprungs for me. I'm grateful my case got dragged out as long as it did. I know it's easier down here. It's got to be. This is all kids. That's seven months I don't have to do in a real joint with adults."

Rikers is a jail, not a prison. Most everybody here is waiting for an outcome to their case. Anybody getting sentenced to more than a year goes upstate to do his time. And there are no adolescents up there, no kiddy playtime. It's all man-on-man.

I wasn't going to tell Sanchez about all the trouble Pops got into upstate, and have him lose any more sleep worrying.

Sanchez ran down what all the COs and teachers were like for me. Then he asked me about my face. I told him I got cut in a fight and stopped it there.

He saw there was nothing in my bucket and asked if I wanted to juggle with Brick.

"I could represent you," he said. "That would help me cut down on what I owe him, before I ship out. I don't need a debt like that following me up north."

I turned him down flat. I wasn't trying to get involved with anything in this house. I was tangled up in enough bullshit already. For the next two weeks, I was willing to be poor. And I wasn't going to let anyone suck me in.

Later, we got a bunch of new jacks in the house. I was happy about that because it gave dudes something to look at besides me.

One of the kids came in with a brand-new hoodie. And after the idiot let on that he'd got locked up for jumping a turn-stile, it was gone. Inmates don't have any respect for a crime like that. He should have just hung a sign around his neck that read, I'M A HERB. TAKE MY SWEATSHIRT.

The dude who took his hoodie didn't even pretend he wanted to borrow it. He just took it right off the kid's back. But that herb didn't have anything else to put on. So he was walking around half the day without a shirt.

"Get your new-jack ass dressed," Ms. Armstrong told him. "You're not at home."

When he couldn't, she knew he'd been jacked.

Ms. Armstrong grabbed an old rag of a shirt from one of the house buckets in the officers' station. Everyone was laughing because they thought she was going to give it to the herb. Instead, she found the robber and made *him* wear that smelly rag for the rest of the day.

That herb got his sweatshirt back and stayed close to Ms. Armstrong until lights-out. He was tied to her so tight, dudes started calling him "Apron Strings."

On Rikers, most dudes wear their own clothes because they're not convicted yet and aren't considered property of the state. But lots of inmates wish they could wear state-issued uniforms.

Wearing your own clothes means you have to fight to keep them. There's always somebody who thinks your threads are better than his. Lots of kids tell their families not to send them good clothes from home. It's not worth the trouble.

Dudes brag about their threads at home and how fly they look when they're on the streets. They say they're going "undercover" on Rikers Island. Corrections won't let you wear a pair of two-hundred-dollar sneakers anyway. That's because they know there's going to be a war over them, and they don't want to have to settle one.

I waited all day to get called out for a visit, but the call never came. This was the first Saturday I hadn't seen my mother since I was locked up. I guess she'd juggled her workdays at Key Food to see me that past Thursday. It had been only two days since she was here, but I missed her bad already.

SUNDAY,
JUNE 7

CHAPTER
18

Around eleven o'clock, most dudes were just waking up. I was already sitting in the dayroom, among the plastic tables and chairs, looking out of the emergency doors. The doors are there in case of a fire or something, and they're never locked—it's a law. You could go charging through them and no CO could stop you. I even daydreamed about doing that, with my feet in high gear and flames shooting out of my ass. But those doors are hooked up to a loud siren. And if you ever did decide to jet, you'd only be out in the yard with a few seconds' head start and nowhere to run.

I watched the mess hall workers, some of them kids from our house, bringing food in from the main building. There's no real kitchen in the Sprungs' mess hall, so the food comes to us already cooked. They wheel it across the yard on pushcarts packed to the top. You can tell what's for lunch by looking at what the workers spill on the way through. Only they never have to clean it up. The seagulls and cats fight each other over that job.

After lunch, me and some other guys watched from the dayroom as the mess hall workers were getting ready to race those same pushcarts back across the yard.

"Speed Racer from Crown Heights, drivin' the Brooklyn Bomb," screamed one kid.

"A hundred twenty-fifth and Lexington Ave. in the house," yelled another one. "Behind the wheel of the Booty Shaker."

We were hyped to see it, and even started making bets on who'd win.

The workers lined their carts up, and then the CO in charge of the mess hall blew his whistle. They took off screeching and hollering, like they were racing go-carts at some special summer camp for kids from the projects. But the two of them reached the far gate at almost the same time, and everybody watching argued for almost an hour over who'd won.

The TV in the dayroom had a full house most of the day.

There's no cable in jail, and that's good because the eight regular channels cause enough drama. Kids are forever arguing over what they're going to watch, and sometimes they'll even juggle for it. Some dudes will really want to see a program, but they'll keep quiet about it. They hope someone else will do the fighting for them or that they'll collect off some herb who wants to see the same show they do.

Asking a dude what TV show he wants to watch in jail is like playing cards. You've got to be able to read his face and keep yours still.

"Violence. Violence. Violence. That's the kind of programs you all are addicted to," lectured Ms. Armstrong. "Like you haven't seen enough of it for *real* in your own lives."

Nobody argued back at her.

Spanish dudes had their TV time, too. Luis represented them for Brick, and he wanted to keep his customers happy. So we watched the Spanish station on the UHF for a few hours. Black kids didn't mind because all the shows on that station had a woman in a tight-fitting, low-cut dress.

That was one language every dude in the house understood.

After Ms. Armstrong got off duty, some kids even put a blanket over their laps, and got busy with a *Susie*. Almost anything that's soft could be a Susie. Most kids get a new rubber glove from the house gang that cleans the floors and bathroom, and they put Vaseline inside it.

Back in Mod-3 one time, a rookie CO pulled the night tour, and dudes thought she was really hot. After lights-out, the beds all started rocking and she didn't know what was happening. Then kids started tossing their Susies up front where she sat in the Plexiglas bubble. When the steady officers found out about it the next morning, they burned the house from commissary for two weeks.

When the COs in Sprung #3 put the phones out that night, I decided to call home. I talked to my grandma and my sisters during slot time, but Mom was visiting a neighbor in the apartment building across the street.

During prime time, Jersey was watching the phones alone, and it was too easy.

"You wanna have to sit on a toilet again?" I asked, as I strolled by him.

He didn't want to fight and I guess he was too embarrassed to call for Brick. I was talking to Mom when Brick's other doldier, Barnett, saw me on the phone. He went over to Jersey and started grilling him.

When I was finished, I walked right past those two clowns and into the dayroom.

MONDAY, JUNE 8

CHAPTER 19

Demarco was waiting in the hallway of the school trailer on Monday morning. He was tossing off kids' first names again as we walked inside, and I was surprised when he called mine.

"Good morning, Martin," he said as I passed.

He must have checked the ID cards in the box on Friday.

That made me want to smile. But I didn't, because I didn't want to look weak in front of anybody there.

Everyone went to their classes, and Demarco was pointing at me and Ritz.

"This way, gentlemen," he said.

We were in his homeroom now, the GED class.

If you prove you can read and write on the placement test, they put you in the GED room. Most kids wanted to be in there because you get more props from the teachers, and it's less like a zoo than the rest of the rooms.

Sanchez and Jersey were in Demarco's class, too. And after my stunt during prime time, Brick had cut Jersey out of his crew the night before.

"I'm in and that Jersey kid's out," Shaky had boasted to the whole north side before lights-out. "I told you I pulled my weight."

Dudes didn't take him serious till he said it within earshot of Brick, who nodded his head.

Demarco started his English class, and we read a story written by a man who'd been locked up for ten years. He wrote about what he would do if he had just one day of freedom: take his twelve-year-old daughter to the park. Then Demarco asked what we would do if Corrections let us go home for just one day. Some kids said they would see their families. Others wanted to be with their girls or homeboys.

"I'd spend the day on my couch eating my grandmother's biscuits and gravy," Jersey said fast, like it was a race. "In Newark, New Jersey—not New York."

It was the first time I'd ever heard Jersey say anything, besides his name that first night in the bathroom. I was surprised at how he sounded. His voice was high and he talked superquick. I had to replay everything he said in my head to slow it down so that I didn't miss any of the words.

"If I had one day off this island, I'd run off and nobody would ever find me again," said Sanchez.

"You can't run away from the world," Demarco told him.

"It's not the world I want to run away from," Sanchez came back. "It's jail!"

Ritz talked about splitting the day in half and seeing his two girlfriends.

"Both of them are pregnant," Ritz said. "So I don't want to choose one over the other."

Then dudes said if they ever found out that either girl was black, they'd kill him.

I didn't have a steady girl, and only Mom came to visit. So I said I'd take her someplace nice for dinner—that I wanted to pay the bill and bring her back and forth by cab, instead of the subway or bus.

Right before Demarco's class was over, there was fussing in the hall right outside the door. Kids ran over to the big plastic window to see what was happening.

The COs had pulled some dude out of class and threw him on the wall. You could tell by the way they dragged him out that he must have really pissed them off.

Demarco was already in the hallway talking to Miss Archer, the math teacher.

Sanchez had told me all about her. She was a dime piece with straight brown hair, and she wore long skirts that showed off the curves of her hips.

A kid from another room snuck over to ours, and he couldn't stop laughing. He said the dude on the wall got caught jerking off to Miss Archer. And that he was really into it when she saw him and called for the COs.

The classrooms are real small, and there's only room for two rows of chairs. So he couldn't have been more than ten feet away when she nailed him.

Someone yelled, "Captain on deck!"

Kids scrambled to get back in their seats, and everybody got silent.

Captain Montenez walked into the trailer and just ripped into the dude. "You lowlife bastard!" he screamed. "You won't be living in my Sprungs much longer!"

By the time the COs were ready to send that dude back to the house to pack up, he was flat-out bawling.

Captains wear white shirts to stand out from the COs, who dress in blue and report to them. I had seen Montenez operate in the building before. He always acted real cool in his captain's duds, until he exploded on you. Montenez was tall and lean. He would wave his arms and scream at dudes until his shirt almost came out of his pants. Then he'd fix himself up and walk off like he owned the jail.

The COs called the whole house into the hallway and we deuced it up.

"Keep your dicks in your pants!" yelled Montenez. "If you masturbate in class, it's a sexual assault on staff. That's not just bing time. That's a new charge. It means you get rearrested, right here on the Island."

Then he paced up and down the line looking for kids to crack a smile or suck their teeth, so he could run them out, too.

The bing is the place they send you when you really fuck up. It's like solitary, and you're locked down twenty-three hours a day, with an hour outside for exercise. But they can't just send you there. They have to write you up and serve you with the papers. Then the bing court captain hears your case, like a judge. It's never fair because he could be good friends with the captain who wrote you up. They give you a chance to tell your side of it, too. But I never heard of an inmate beating his case. Once you're there, you're guilty. Plain and simple.

We went back into the classroom, and Demarco came with us. It was Miss Archer's time to rotate into our room and teach us math, but she was still in the hall with Montenez.

"I don't know what that dude was thinking," some kid said. "She's *my* girl."

A couple of us laughed low, and Demarco said, "Wait here, I'll tell the captain she's yours!"

The kid begged him not to and nearly freaked when Demarco walked out the door. But Demarco only crossed over to teach his next class, shooting us all a big smile through the window when he got there.

Miss Archer came in and put some math problems on the board. She didn't look half as shook as I thought she would be.

Right away, kids tried to make her feel better.

"That dude played you too dirty," one kid told her. "He's lucky that he got packed up or we woulda put a beating on him for you tonight."

"That's just stupid talk," Miss Archer said. "Please, never hurt anyone over me. All right? He shouldn't get rearrested for that either. And I'll speak to the captain about it later."

I heard that out of her mouth and wondered how she could stand teaching in jail, where everybody was beat down and had been arrested for something.

CHAPTER
20

Besides Officer Carter, our steady COs during the day were Dawson and Arrigo. They were both white, too, but I liked their act because they told you what they wanted up front. The first time you fucked up, they'd talk to you.

"Tell me what you did wrong, kid," Dawson would say, playing good cop.

"Now, what do you think we should do about that?" Arrigo would follow, cracking his knuckles.

The next time, they smacked you around. So when they hit you, they figured you had no one to blame but yourself.

Dawson was tall and thick, and leaned off to one side when he walked. Arrigo was short, with greasy black hair and arms like steam shovels. He showed them off every chance he got and had a tattoo on his right bicep that read, TNT.

"You don't want to get hit with dynamite," Arrigo would tell kids.

The Department of Corrections has signs up that say inmates are in their "care and custody." But most COs would rather keep you *near and in fear.*

Arrigo came to the classroom door during math with Miss Archer and screamed, "Forty, clinic!"

I went into the hallway and waited at the officers' desk for an escort.

There were always kids in the hall that had been thrown out of class. Mr. Murray, that crooked-nosed history teacher, would toss most of them for total bullshit.

Instead of having inmates hold up the wall, Dawson and Arrigo liked to play games. They had one called "London Bridge" for kids who wanted to fight each other. Any pair caught beefing had to lean as far forward as they could, forehead to forehead. Then they had to sing "London Bridge Is Falling Down."

After five minutes of that crap, kids would be begging to make up and go back to class.

They had Barnett and Shaky out there playing patty-cake, Rikers-style.

"You act like babies, we'll treat you like babies," Dawson said. "Now do it again till you both get it right."

Barnett was pissed because Shaky kept screwing up the crossover and missing Barnett's hand.

I watched them do it four times and loved every one.

Patty-cake, patty-cake, legal aid
Get me off Rikers or don't get paid

Do it for my mama, do it for my girl
I gotta make money out in the world.

Some COs would go easy on Brick and his crew because they helped keep the house in line. But Dawson and Arrigo played them the same as everybody else. And the other kids respected that.

The principal, Ms. Jackson, walked through the hall with her high heels tapping the floor, looking into all the classrooms. She was mad because there were kids sleeping in every class.

"You can't allow them to sleep," she pecked at Dawson and Arrigo. "It doesn't look good."

"If they're not bothering anybody, we're not gonna mess with them," Arrigo snapped back.

"This isn't some kind of prep school. These kids have problems," Dawson piped in. "Why don't you just tell your teachers to be more interesting? Maybe that'll help keep them awake."

Only Ms. Jackson didn't break a smile at that and snipped, "I see I'll have to bring this issue to the captain again, maybe even higher up."

Then she banged on a classroom window, pointing inside.

"That one!" she screamed through the hard plastic.

The teacher sent the kid out, and Ms. Jackson motioned him over to the officers' desk as she stormed out of the trailer.

The kid rubbed the sleep out of his eyes and asked the officers, "What I do?"

"Go back to class and try to stay awake," Dawson told him.

"The principal's got her period again. That's what you did," Arrigo said, annoyed.

When I got to the clinic, I had to wait for a doctor to check my stitches. Other inmates were waiting, too.

One dude told me that he'd got sliced all the way down his arm about a week ago.

I thought something like that was better than getting cut on the face. At least he could wear a long-sleeve shirt and keep it covered. But he said that he was in pain every time he had to bend his arm.

A nurse took the bandages off my face and cleaned the cut with some stuff that burned.

"There, that's not too bad," she said with some sympathy. Only I couldn't tell if she meant the burning or my stitches.

That nurse was pretty and having her look over my face made me start to think. I didn't know how shorties out in the world would react to the scar. I also didn't want to walk around having to front and act hard all the time. I didn't know if you could go easy with a cut on your face, without looking like a big-time herb.

"These stitches were put in perfectly. It's almost a shame to remove them. But it's been six days, and they've done their job," said a doctor, who pulled out all fifty-three of them with a small pair of scissors. "I know the physician on duty that day. You were very lucky to get him. Hopefully, his skill will lessen the potential for scarring."

I was nervous to have the sharp edges of those scissors right up against my face. And I gripped both my hands around the sides of the examination table beneath me as I felt the threads pulling through my skin.

I wasn't sure if I could believe him about how it was going to look, or that other doctor. People who work in jail are always covering up for each other.

But at least it felt good to hear.

When that doctor was done, he gave me a legit hand mirror to see for myself. I held it up to my face and saw the smooth, raised line, maybe four inches long, running down my right cheek. And I knew it was a mark that would stay with me forever, like everything else that had touched me on Rikers Island.

He put new bandages on and told me to leave them for a few days. But I was tired of how they made my face feel heavy, so I took them off on the way back to the Sprungs and left them in a trash bin in the main corridor.

Everyone stared when they first saw me. But that wore off pretty quick, probably because they'd seen enough cuts on kids' faces before.

That night Brick came up to me in the house.

"Yo, Forty. I hear you used the phone on my private time. I'll have to start you an account," he said, walking away without waiting for an answer.

It didn't pay for him to press me too much. He had almost everything in the house locked down tight. Right now, I was the only joker in the deck. And he didn't need to chance me flipping the script on him.

TUESDAY, JUNE 9

CHAPTER
21

In English class, Demarco broke us up into groups of four. I was working with Sanchez, Ritz, and Jersey. Each group got a different photo to look over. Ours was a black-and-white picture of a boy swinging on a tire that was hanging from a tree branch. The boy was wearing a cowboy hat and six-shooters, and he had a big smile on his face.

I looked at that picture and started to feel sick. I just wanted not to worry anymore, like that boy.

"What's this got to do with us? We're not in kindergarten," groaned Jersey.

But Demarco shook him off and told each group to make a list of reasons why the person in the picture seemed so happy.

"He's happy 'cause he don't know any better," smirked Sanchez.

"Write that down if that's what you believe," said Demarco. "I want only one answer sheet per group."

That's when Sanchez pushed the pencil and paper toward Ritz, who didn't argue about doing the writing.

"He's happy 'cause he's in his own backyard," said Jersey. "Nothin' can happen to him there. No New York po-lice to set his ass up."

"He's just a kid. He doesn't have to worry about anything," said Sanchez, scratching at his mustache.

Ritz stopped writing and said, "You can't get locked up for cap guns."

"At least a white boy can't," added Jersey.

I said he was happy because somebody wanted to take his picture for something good, not for a jail ID card.

Then Demarco asked us to give the boy advice on how to stay happy when he got older.

We decided that he should stay away from drugs and be serious in school. We laughed at saying that kind of crap, because none of us had ever listened to that rap, even after hearing it a million times.

I wanted to put in something about staying close to his family. But the time ran out and Demarco collected our work. I just kept staring at that picture till I finally folded it up and put it in my pocket.

Miss Archer came in looking at Ritz and me like she'd never seen us before.

"When did the two of you arrive in class?" she asked.

I guess she was too occupied with putting on a good front yesterday, after that kid did her dirty. She added our names to her roll book and wanted to know what kind of math we'd done out in the world.

I told her I was finished with everything in the eleventh grade.

"I'm not sure," Ritz said. "I know I'm solid up to the part where numbers change into letters, like X and Y."

"Yeah, it's fucked up the way math changes into Chinese," somebody said.

"That's why all those Chinese dudes are so good at it," said Sanchez.

And lots of kids agreed with him.

I could see Miss Archer was getting all uptight with kids talking like that.

She started us doing examples from a worksheet.

Dudes kept asking her to work the problems out on the board. And every time she turned around to write, the whole class stopped to look at her ass. Some kid even knocked the eraser down. But Miss Archer never bent over to pick it up. She just wiped the board clean with her hand.

It was like she knew, but just played it off. And it always felt like she was still in control, and could take care of herself.

Kids wanted to know if she saved the dude who got caught jerking off from getting a new charge.

"I wrote up what happened because I had to," Miss Archer said. "But I'm not happy with the way the captain's pushing it. And no matter what, I won't go to court against that boy."

Three more teachers came to our room that day after Miss Archer.

I'd missed them all my first day when I went to the clinic.

Mrs. Daniels, an older lady, was the science teacher, and it was like being in class with your grandmother.

If you said *fuck*, or *nigger*, she'd be all over you.

Kids took her serious and even stopped each other from cursing.

She had a big card on her desk with an *F* on one side and an *N* on the other. If you slipped up and said one of those two words, she'd flash the card at you and keep right on teaching.

Kids would get her to talk about how the COs hit us anytime they wanted.

"It's not right," she said. "I can't stand it. I've discussed it with the other teachers and our principal. If nothing changes, one day I'm going to do something about it myself."

While the class was working, Mrs. Daniels sat down right next to me.

"You want to tell me about what happened to you?" she asked. "And what about your family?"

I didn't say much because I didn't want other dudes to hear.

"Just jail stuff," I told her.

But I appreciated her sitting in the chair next to me like that, even though she was a bit of a pain.

It's hard to find people in jail who say they're worried about you. I guess that's why other dudes put up with her, too, and showed her mad respect.

Mr. Murray was the next teacher. As soon as he walked in, Mrs. Daniels touched a kid on the head who was sleeping. The kid opened his eyes to see Murray and woke right up. The whole feeling in the room changed when he got there. Everybody got stiff, and it was like having one of the COs in class.

"Can you explain how that photo-synth-esis works again?" some dude asked Mrs. Daniels.

Murray made a noise in his throat and tapped on his watch.

"I'll go over it again tomorrow," she said.

Then Mrs. Daniels picked up her books and said good-bye to the class. But she and Murray never said a word to each other.

Murray pushed his little glasses back toward the bridge of his crooked nose and handed out thick history textbooks without any covers.

"Corrections takes the hard covers off so we can't use the books to beat somebody over the head," Sanchez whispered to me.

Murray wrote on the blackboard, "Read chapter 8 and answer all questions on page 179," using a chalk holder so he wouldn't get his hands dirty. His letters were small and straight, like he was using lines on the board that no one else could see.

"Do the assignment while I check the work in your folders," he said.

I didn't have a folder. But I wasn't going to say anything to him unless he talked to me first. Dudes just sat there quiet, reading and answering questions from the book. Only no one looked happy about it.

Sanchez had told me that Murray never taught a lesson. He just wrote down what pages to look at in the book. The GED class had it easier with Murray because everybody knew how to read and write. But in the dumber classes, kids got bored and would start to screw up. Then Murray would pitch a fit and kick them out.

Murray went over the answers with us. But he only knew one kid's name in the class, and that was Jessup.

Dudes called Jessup "Toothpick" because he was skinny like a rail. And some of them wanted to snap him in two because of the way he sucked up to Murray.

"Toothpick needs one history class to graduate high school," whispered Sanchez. "So he's always showing Murray how much work and extra credit bullshit he's doing."

Murray called on me for one of the answers.

"You there," he said, pointing at my face.

I read him the answer straight from the book, and then it hit me what Demarco had said about names. And it felt like Murray really had just called me "*Table*" or "*Chair*."

At the end of class, Ritz and me decided to put our work into Sanchez's folder, just to not talk to Murray.

Lunch was next, and when we got back from the mess hall, Mr. Rowe was already in our room. He was a short, old white man, with even whiter hair. Dudes grabbed worksheets off his desk, but no one paid any attention to them. Sanchez said to hold one just in case the principal or the captain came walking through.

Mr. Rowe just let us sit and talk. He wasn't even busy

doing something else, like reading a newspaper. He just sat there quiet, staring off into space. I finally looked at the worksheet and saw that Mr. Rowe taught life skills.

We ended the day in the computer room. The man that ran the place wasn't a teacher.

"I'm a paraprofessional," he said. "I don't get paid to teach, so I don't."

There was no Internet connection, and those computers looked old enough to come from the Stone Age.

The man handed everybody a book of lessons, but most kids knew the code to get into the games. Jersey was that man's helper, and he hooked me up.

Jersey didn't seem to hold anything against me. I even started to like him, since we were in class together and he was on the outs with Brick.

I played solitaire and Pac-Man.

Dudes were wild to play some computer game where you're an ace detective. You chase a lady spy named Carmen Sandiego all over the world, trying to put her in jail. I didn't know why they liked that game so much. They were all pissed off that some cop did that to them for real and dropped them on Rikers Island.

That night I was sitting on my bed talking with Sanchez. When it got quiet, I took the picture of that boy on the swing out of my pocket and looked it over again.

I said, "I wish I could go back in time and be that age," and then tears started down Sanchez's face.

Tears are nothing new in jail. Dudes cry all the time on

Rikers Island and nobody makes fun of them. A kid could be laughing and joking with everybody one minute, then crying by himself the next. Sometimes the stress is too much and it breaks you.

I cried a couple of times back in Mod-3, after I didn't go home from court. But I got past all that, and a lot of those feelings just got hard.

"My moms died of pneumonia last year, and there's nobody left I'm close with," said Sanchez. "I remember my father being a real prick, and with any luck he's dead someplace."

I'd seen lots of kids like Sanchez on Rikers Island without anywhere to go. But he was doing the best out of all of them, and even had his GED.

He kept talking about going upstate and how it had him worried.

"Things are different with adults," he said through the tears. "There, you've got to watch your back and your ass. If you need protection, you become somebody's boy. Then he can do what he wants to you, or even rent you out."

I couldn't understand why he was so shook. Sanchez held his own in the Sprungs without being anybody's doldier or Maytag. But he had it in his head that he was going to get ripped off—raped—upstate.

Adolescents on Rikers Island don't run that game. Dudes with that kind of juice here want to prove how tough they are or how many girls they've got out in the world waiting for them.

Besides getting cut, the worst thing that can happen to you on Rikers Island is washing some thug's socks and drawers every day. I'd never heard of any kid getting ripped off in an adolescent house. Dudes make fun of that shit to no end. They call it "taking your peanut butter."

Even kids who still sucked their thumbs were safe with other adolescents. But everybody knew it was a different world upstate. When adults are in the middle of serving real time and get hard up, things change. They probably do shit there that you couldn't pay them to do out in the world.

Ritz walked past and saw me holding the picture of that boy.

"We doing extra on that assignment for Demarco?" he asked.

He saw Sanchez drying his eyes but never said anything about it. Then Ritz went off and came back with Jersey. We were all looking at that picture of the kid swinging from a tree and smiling in his fake-ass cowboy duds. It was hard to believe, but we were doing homework on Rikers Island.

The last time I did homework was in my real house. And I don't think I ever sat around with three other dudes doing schoolwork outside of class before, not even in a library.

Brick saw us all together and came over with his doldiers, Luis and Barnett.

"So you guys think you're the new shit?" he said.

He pointed to each of us, shooting off a list of complaints.

"You owe me for the phone. You can't hold your weight. You're gonna pay your tab before you ship up north. And white boy better hope he don't get run out of this house," Brick said in one long breath.

Right then, I could feel his power start to slip away from him. I could hear it in his voice.

"We're still running *my* game," warned Brick. "Don't get any ideas that you bums can hold it down around here."

WEDNESDAY, JUNE 10

CHAPTER 22

The next day in school, dudes were trying to follow the life skills teacher, Mr. Rowe, from class to class. He had the VCR and was showing an animal video with tigers and lions hunting in the jungle. It was like spending the day at the movies, and dudes were willing to do anything for a seat.

Both Dawson and Arrigo had the day off, so Officer Carter, the dude who'd used his money as a napkin to taunt us, was running the show with a woman CO who looked like she'd stepped out of a beauty parlor.

She had long nails and big hair, and spent most of her time on the phone. And I could tell right away that she thought that she was better than us.

"I don't want to hear a thing out of your mouths that doesn't start with 'Excuse me, officer,'" she told us.

Kids were scared of Carter and wouldn't jump between rooms. They didn't want to risk getting thrown on the wall and kicked in the ass. Instead, they put pressure on Mr. Rowe to take them with him. He'd push the VCR through the hall, and dudes would bang on the windows and come to the doors begging to go along.

Please, Mr. Rowe. I'm your best student.

You promised me last time, remember?

This is my last day. I'm getting shipped upstate.

Carter would karate-kick every door that cracked open when someone tried to peek at what was going on, and he almost took some kid's nose off when one slammed shut.

Then two quiet kids who mostly got herbed by everybody else started a fight over the last seat in Demarco's room.

Dudes put a battery in one of their backs, saying, "If you fold up to that little shit, you really are a herb."

The two kids both took boxing stances with a pencil in each fist, the points sticking out. Dudes were standing on their chairs cheering like they had front-row seats at Madison Square Garden. But the two kids only danced around each other for a while.

"Keep dreaming, sweethearts," mocked Carter, as he dragged them both by the collar into the hall.

They sat crying on the floor after Carter threatened to write them up and ship them off to the main building.

The Sprungs housed lots of kids charged with petty bull-shit. If your classification was too high and you were looking at something like a murder charge or armed robbery, you had to live in the main building. I guess Corrections figured that being outside so close to the fence and bay would tempt dudes facing big time.

So when a kid fucked up in the Sprungs, all a CO had to do was threaten to ship his ass to the building. They'd get all scared and turn to jelly. That's why it was easy for a thug like Brick to push these kids around.

I had a low classification, but got sent to Mod-3 in the main anyway. I had to put up with more shit from *real* thugs, but I got off that scared routine pretty quick.

Carter went on break and a big CO I recognized from the building held down his spot. Kids like to always know which COs are on duty. This way they can figure out what they can get away with, and what games to play.

Now both COs were just covering other posts. Neither of them knew what classrooms kids belonged to, and we started to bounce between rooms like a herd of kangaroos.

That big CO must have been doing overtime off the midnight tour. He was sound asleep at the desk when Murray stepped into the hallway.

"Officer, I want you to remove this *miscreant* from my classroom," announced Murray, pointing to Shaky.

The woman CO went over to Murray's door and told Shaky to step out. But Shaky tried to play her off and wouldn't even get out of his seat.

"Maybe you don't listen to your mother, but you'll listen to me!" she went off, pulling Shaky out of Murray's room by his shirtsleeve.

Then she told him to get on the wall, and he finally did after walking around the hall for a while. She cursed his mother for not listening right away, and he cursed hers back.

"What did you say to me?" she screamed.

"I said, '*Your* mother.'"

The big man raised his head from the desk and hollered, "Watch your mouth, son. If I have to get up, I'll slap you a new one!"

The woman CO walked over to Shaky and out of nowhere threw a wild punch past his head. The two of them got tangled up and started to wrestle on the floor. She landed a couple of good shots and her partner went charging over there.

Kids were all pressed up against the windows and doors of their classrooms to watch. The big man grabbed Shaky from the pile and slammed him back against the wall, twisting his arm behind him hard.

Everybody thought it was over for Shaky. It should have meant bing time, after those COs wrote up what happened *their way.*

But it all changed fast.

The woman CO kept jawing with Shaky.

"You think you know who you are. I'll teach you," she said. "You're a damn inmate."

Shaky was all upset, and the spit was flying from his mouth.

"No, I'll teach you," he said back. "Bitch!"

That's when she just lost it.

She took the fire extinguisher from behind the desk and ran at him. I thought she was going to hit him over the head with it, but she turned it over and soaked him good instead.

Some dudes were rolling on the floor laughing, but others were burning mad.

Both Demarco and Mrs. Daniels were standing in the hall in front of their classrooms.

That woman CO knew she'd screwed up, and after a while she sent Shaky back to class. He sat there the rest of the morning, dripping wet.

When Carter got back, the teachers told him what happened.

He took that woman CO off to the side and had some quiet words with her.

Then I couldn't believe what happened next.

Carter called Shaky out and said his partner wanted to talk to him.

"Look. I lost my head. I'm sorry," she apologized.

Kids had never heard anything like that from a CO before and didn't know what to make of it. Shaky was just glad not to get written up.

After lunch, Carter was on duty with Ms. Armstrong.

That woman CO came back and set Shaky up in the computer room with Chinese food. He was sitting there like a king eating beef and broccoli.

The COs canceled computer class while he was in there and wouldn't let anyone else in the room. Brick was wild that one of his crew had scored big and he couldn't get his cut.

"That CO could lose her job over what she did," said Demarco.

And Mrs. Daniels was trying to get the other teachers as witnesses against her.

Big Johnson came on duty at four, and you could tell from his walk that he was steamed over something. He swung his arms more than usual and dropped his shoulder like he would smack anything that moved.

Before we went to supper he deuced up both sides of the house at the front door. Sometimes when a CO wants to give a speech he has to wait for everyone to settle down. But no one was even thinking about making a sound with him in that kind of mood.

"The captain says this house looks like a pigsty!" snarled Johnson. "And if I got it figured right, that makes me a pig farmer! Now does anyone here want to explain to me how I turned from a corrections officer into a fuckin' pig farmer in his eyes?"

Johnson fired half the house gang that does the cleaning and called the others "no good slackers." Jersey kept his cleaning job but heard it from Johnson because the clothes he'd washed were still drying on the vents from last night.

"I'll put this house on permanent burn if you slobs can't get it clean," threatened Johnson.

No house wants to lose its privileges. That means no commissary, no extra phone time, and no TV. It would be just jail and school.

After supper, on the way back to the house, Johnson lined

us up outside the mess hall. Captain Montenez was standing off to the side. But some of the kids didn't see him there and were horsing around.

This dude from the south side was standing five feet off the line, drinking a milk.

Johnson called his name and the dude mumbled, "Yes, sir," without even taking his lips from the carton.

"Yes, *son*? You called me *son*?" raged Johnson.

Then Johnson ran up to that dude and smacked him across the mouth.

The dude was stunned. His mouth was hanging open and milk was dripping down his face like his mama had just popped him off her tit.

"So I'm your *son* now?" Johnson kept on. "Explain that."

"I said *sir*," the dude pleaded. "Not *son*. *Sir*."

But Johnson didn't want to hear it.

Then Captain Montenez stepped in and told the dude that there was no food allowed outside the mess hall. He said if the dude wasn't drinking a milk in the wrong place, there wouldn't have been a problem.

"Nice work," Montenez told Johnson as he lit a cigarette. "Now if you can just keep that house clean, I'll be satisfied."

When we got back to the house, *everyone* was cleaning, not just the house gang. The COs took the antenna off the TV in the dayroom, so you knew they were serious. Kids were either mopping the floor or cleaning the bathroom with scrub brushes.

"I'll pound the shit out of anyone who doesn't pull his weight and gets us burned," warned Brick.

He had the most to lose, because it would cut into his business big-time.

I was scrubbing sinks in the bathroom with Ritz.

There's work you do in jail that you would never even think about doing at home. Mom and Grandma did work like that every week for my sisters and me. I never once helped them. But there I was, cleaning for Johnson so he could get himself a gold star.

All of a sudden, I heard jawing, and saw Barnett and Luis shoving Jersey around in the far end of the bathroom. I jumped up and went over before they screwed it up for everybody. I was surprised when Ritz followed behind me.

Then Brick walked in and we were all crowded together.

Everyone had a grip on a mop or a brush, except for Brick.

I could see by their faces that his goons didn't like the numbers. They were used to better odds and waited for Brick to make a stand.

"So you're their leader now? All up in *my* business!" Brick shouted at me.

It was just noise and no action. He had every chance to set it off and didn't. Then Ms. Armstrong marched inside to see what was going on.

"Better drop those attitudes," she demanded.

And we all went back to cleaning.

THURSDAY, JUNE 11

CHAPTER
23

O n our way across the yard the next morning, a family of
cats followed us to the school trailer. The teachers weren't
there, so we had to wait outside for them. They'd got
caught up in an alarm in the main building and there wasn't
any movement through the jail. Miss Archer usually fed the
cats in the morning before school, and they were waiting, too.

Families of cats live underneath the school trailers in the
Sprungs, and most kids like having them around. The cats
would stretch out in the sun on the hot concrete, like they
owned the place. Seeing them made dudes think about their
pets back home.

"My moms had to give my dog away 'cause there was no
one to walk him," some kid said. "That cuts to the heart."

Sanchez said that whenever a cat died under the trailer,
all the classrooms smelled like dead cat. It happened twice the
month before, so the captain gave the order that they had to go

and that nobody was allowed to feed them anymore. But that didn't stop Miss Archer or the mess hall workers from putting out scraps. And I knew the only ones 100 percent happy to see the cats go would be the rats.

The teachers finally were escorted out to the Sprungs, and kids gave them a little cheer.

"Sometimes we're locked down, too," said Demarco, heading into the trailer ahead of us.

We'd lost most of our time with Demarco waiting outside. But he put a word puzzle on the board while he got all his things together.

"I'm not into school today, Demarco," said some quiet kid from the south side. "I feel sick to my stomach."

"Put your head down and rest awhile," Demarco told him. "Maybe you'll start to feel better."

On Rikers, you can't get out of school by being sick. When the house travels, the COs can't leave you behind, because there's no one left to watch you. Sick call isn't until ten o'clock. Besides, you'd have to be bleeding or half dead before the COs sent you to the clinic. There's just too much paperwork involved.

The pain I was feeling on the right side of my face was mostly down to a whisper. And I had to check myself from running my fingers over the scar, feeling for it all the time.

Kids asked Demarco why he stood in the hall while that woman CO beat on Shaky and didn't do anything to stop it. They wanted to know if he was going to report her to the deputy warden, like Mrs. Daniels.

"I always want to be out there when something happens," Demarco said, superserious. "Somewhere in the back of their minds, the COs know we're watching and hold back. Teachers make good witnesses. That's why the COs like it so much when we write you guys up. But Shaky's still in one piece. So I'm not going to get crazy over this. If I did, the powers that run this place would find a way to ship me out. And I don't know what kind of teacher would come to take my place."

The principal shoved open the door, screaming at that sick kid Demarco told to put his head down, "You've got to be awake, young man! Get up right now or else! And you keep him awake, Mr. Costa! That's *your* job!"

Demarco took a deep breath and turned away. Then all of a sudden he just blew.

"You don't care what his problem is or what he's about, do you?" popped Demarco.

"Mr. Costa," she interrupted.

But Demarco kept right on going.

"All you know is that when his head's down *you* don't look good!" he hollered, chasing her back into the hallway.

The two of them disappeared into the teachers' room making all kinds of noise. Dawson and Arrigo were laughing hysterical over it.

"I told you. This school shit is better than any soap opera on TV," Dawson told his partner.

There are lots of reasons an adolescent might sleep through the day on Rikers Island. He could be stressed about his case and the time that's hanging over his head. He might have a problem with his family at home, or his girl, or his baby. A dude with a baby is always taking heat from his baby's mom because she's doing all the work while he's locked down.

Some herbs are under so much pressure from thugs, they might even be afraid to sleep at night when the house is dark. So they do the Rip van Winkle during the day when it's light and the COs can see more.

I couldn't understand why the principal got so uptight about kids sleeping in class. It's not like you could hold school on Rikers Island and make the jail part go away.

Ms. Jackson was black, but it was like she didn't know anything about us. That's why dudes called her "Ms. Jerk-off." The black COs like Johnson and Ms. Armstrong were part of the system and *had* to play you for an inmate. But she was supposed to be there to help kids. Go figure.

"If we were out in the world, the principal would never act like that," said Jersey. "Only with these cops to watch her back."

"You don't get it," said Sanchez. "We're not students to her, just inmates."

Maybe that's why Demarco didn't get along with her. He saw us as people, and not total fuckups.

We were doing math with Miss Archer when a black staff member I hadn't seen before called Sanchez out of the room. Other dudes wanted to go, too, and a couple of them even begged.

"You know what, I'm here for everybody," said the man, without bending an inch to that pressure. "But right now it's this young man's turn. If there's time today, I'll be back for a few more."

I was surprised when the COs let him and Sanchez walk right out of the trailer. Jersey told me the man's name was Green, and that he was a guidance counselor, just like in a real high school.

"Mr. Green's got an office in the next trailer," said Jersey. "He'll bless you and let you use the phone to call your family or lawyer. He done his own bid upstate, too, and tells kids what to expect when they get there."

I didn't know that you could have a police record and still get a job like that in a school. Maybe that Mr. Green should have been explaining about kids on Rikers Island to Ms. Jerk-off. But I was happy Sanchez had somebody he could talk to. Maybe he'd start to feel less stressed.

CHAPTER
24

When it was time for history, Murray sat at the corner of the desk closest to the door, looking out at us over his glasses. I'd had mean son-of-a-bitch teachers like him out in the world before. But I couldn't understand why he was here. If he hated kids like us so much, why would he come to work on Rikers Island?

Some dudes said it was because we were locked up and nobody cared if he taught us anything. Other kids said he'd be nothing without the COs. That he'd get his ass kicked in a regular school without that kind of protection.

On my first trip to court, I counted eleven gates from the main corridor in the building to the other end of the bridge. The steel door out to the Sprungs and the checkpoint in the yard made thirteen. Murray passed through those gates every damn day. But why? There had to be some high school in the city that would take his sorry ass—one that was easier to get to than this floating rock.

We were reading about the Trojan Horse. How these Greek soldiers hid in its big, wooden belly and came out after the dumb Trojans pulled it inside the gates of Troy. Kids read that story and started talking about how they could sneak off Rikers Island.

"What would you do if a helicopter showed up in the yard and dropped down one of those ladders made out of rope?" asked Jersey, out of nowhere.

Kids swore they'd climb right up, even if they didn't know who was flying it.

"No way," answered Ritz. "It'd probably be a setup. The COs outside the gates with guns would shoot you down."

Even Murray had a smile on his face and listened to the whole rap before he snapped, "Enough of this nonsense. Back to work."

There were more ways to talk about escaping in the Sprungs because it's all out in the open. From where the water starts, maybe it's a half mile across to LaGuardia Airport. Before that, there are two fifteen-foot-high fences between the Sprungs and the hill down to the bay. They're both strung with razor wire, all the way across the top. So even if you threw a blanket over the wire on the first fence, the second might cut you bad enough to make you turn back.

Some dudes swore there was even razor wire under the water. They said that Corrections hid it there in case you made it far enough to swim. But I didn't know how they could string it underwater or keep it from rusting.

I looked up and suddenly Murray was collecting all his books early, before the end of class.

"Pass them up to my desk quickly," he said.

Then Murray stepped outside, calling over Dawson and Arrigo.

They talked for a minute, and then the three of them walked back inside looking us over.

Dawson said, "If you have it, give it back now."

Nobody moved a muscle.

I saw Dawson look at one of his snitches from the north side. But the dude's eyes just rolled in his head to say he didn't know what was going on.

"Are you sure you had it when you walked into this room?" Arrigo asked Murray, annoyed.

Murray stood there silent with his arms folded across his chest, nodding.

The COs finally let on that they were looking for the chalk holder Murray used when he wrote on the board. It was made of metal, so they weren't going to just let it disappear.

Leave it to that piss-ass Murray not to get his hands dirty with chalk. Instead, he walks around Rikers Island with a big-time piece of contraband, waiting for some kid to rob him.

"We're gonna leave you boys for a minute to think about this," said Arrigo.

Then the COs left the room and made Murray go, too. They knew we'd put pressure on each other to give the stupid thing up.

Jersey was the first to beat the drum.

"Just give it up and get these damn po-lice off our backs," he said.

Dudes threatened to kick the shit out of any kid who'd snatched it.

Only no one came clean.

The COs stepped back inside and searched the floor and in the corners, just in case somebody got scared and tossed it. Then they searched us one by one at the door.

We put our hands on the wall and Dawson patted us down. Arrigo made the rest of us keep our hands on our heads so we couldn't pass the chalk holder off if it was still in the room. Dawson was really getting pissed. And you could hear it in his voice every time he yelled, "Next!"

All the while, crooked-nosed Murray was in the hall watching through the window. When the chalk holder didn't turn up in our room, the COs went from class to class. They gave the same speech and patted down every inmate in the house.

Brick sneaked over to our room ready to blow.

"If you bastards get my business shut down over this, I'm gonna kill somebody," he threatened us.

Some kid promised Brick that no one in our class took it.

That made me sick to hear. You never feed a thug's head like that.

Then Brick looked me right in the face and said, "You got to keep your misfit crew in check, Forty. All you're gonna do is get the rest of these GED nerds in trouble."

I was just glad Ritz and Jersey played it silent. If Brick was going to talk up that we were a crew, I wanted kids to think we stood together.

It was time for lunch, but we weren't going anywhere. Dawson and Arrigo called Captain Montenez, and he showed up with a fresh bunch of COs.

That's when I knew this shit was going to get deep.

Montenez called the mess hall workers from our house back to the trailer. Then he had a fit because Dawson and Arrigo forgot about Sanchez being next door with the counselor. And when Sanchez and the mess hall workers came up clean, too, Montenez got serious, ordering the COs to strip-search the kids in each classroom.

The COs went into the rooms while Montenez stood at the door. We pushed all the chairs and desks to the middle of the floor. Then we had to take off all our clothes and throw them into one big pile.

I was standing in a classroom full of kids with my hands against the wall, naked.

The COs patted down our clothes and went through all the pockets. They mostly found food and cigarettes, and con- fiscated it all. You weren't allowed to bring any of that shit to school, but dudes tried to puff in the bathroom and sneak food into class anyway. Then they found some kid's pussy maga- zine rolled up in his sleeve.

"If this is sticky and I touch it, I'm gonna hammer whoever it belongs to," sneered Arrigo.

Demarco was going from room to room, talking to kids and

looking for the chalk holder. Mrs. Daniels was helping, too, but she disappeared when they made us take off our clothes. Murray and Ms. Jackson were standing around at the officers' desk taking heat from Montenez.

"The two of you graduated college, right?" ripped the captain. "I guess you could be smart and stupid at the same time, bringing a metal chalk holder in here."

Miss Archer had been on a break, and no one told her what was going on.

"Oh my God!" she screamed, as she walked into the trailer and saw a whole class standing naked.

Some of the COs were laughing hard over it.

"That's not funny," said Ms. Armstrong, punching Arrigo in the arm.

I wasn't surprised the COs couldn't dig up Murray's piece. Usually when a kid swipes something, other inmates see it go down. Then word gets around. If there's too much heat the kid gets ratted out. But most dudes in our room didn't even remember seeing Murray with the chalk holder that day. Never mind robbing him for it.

"Get these inmates dressed and take 'em to lunch," ordered Montenez.

Maybe he didn't *want* to do it, but it was the rules. Montenez had to feed us before a certain time, no matter what.

School was canceled in the afternoon, and Sprung #3 was officially on the burn.

CHAPTER
25

Back at the house, the COs took the count. I could hear defeat in the voice of every kid as they counted off. It was like we'd just been whipped in a fight that we didn't even know was coming.

There are always fights in jail, and mostly it's over something that matters to someone. But nobody wanted to be on the burn over Murray's stupid chalk holder.

"I don't even believe one of you guys swiped it," said Dawson.

"Too bad it don't matter what we think. The captain says it happened," said Arrigo. "Maybe they'll bring *the chair* out for everybody to sit in."

Arrigo meant that maybe a kid boofed it.

Corrections has an electronic chair they make you sit in, and it'll buzz if you jammed any metal inside of you. The COs can't make you give it up or go get it themselves. They're not allowed to. They can just isolate you from everybody else. But I couldn't imagine some kid sticking a piece of metal that big up his ass.

Lots of doldiers boof razor blades in case they have to go to war. They wrap them up in wads of toilet paper so they won't cut themselves. The only problem is that if a fight jumps off fast you can't get to your stash right away. You have to shit it out first.

After supper, Johnson didn't put the phones out. He was trying to squeeze us and maybe look like a supercop if the piece turned up on his tour.

"The dayroom's off-limits," Johnson ordered. "Sit at your beds. I want quiet time till lights-out."

The only movement was for the bathroom and the house gang cleaning up. It was four hours of just sitting on our beds looking at each other. Only a couple of dudes went to sleep. Most of us were too pissed off for that.

I looked at the face of every inmate on our side. There were thirty-two other black faces, sixteen Spanish ones, and Ritz.

To see us locked up like that, you'd think black and Spanish people were nothing but scum. None of us believed that was true. But it didn't make us feel any better about ourselves either.

Ritz got called out on a visit and he was all smiles. He walked down the rows of beds with his hands curved over his stomach, like a pregnant woman.

"I never know which one of my girls it is," he whispered. "But it don't matter. It's the same with both of them."

Ritz wasn't even sure which one was due first. Dudes told him that if he gave both babies the same name he'd never mess up and call out the wrong one. He liked that trick and decided on "Chris" because it worked for a boy or a girl.

Some kids used the time to write letters. You never think much about writing out in the world because you can see people and the phone is always there. But when you're locked up letters become important. You write to people and sometimes they write back. Some dudes get pictures from home of things they missed, like their baby's birthday party. Other kids get pictures of their girls in bathing suits and pass them around to show off.

I watched Sanchez for a while. He was lying down with a pillow over his face. I could tell he wasn't really asleep by the way he was breathing. It would change all the time from fast to slow. You watch lots of kids sleep when you're locked up, and they always breathe steady.

"How can you lie there for so long without moving?" I asked low.

He lifted the pillow off his face and answered, "Man, I'm already part dead."

Quiet time was hardest for Shaky because he couldn't sit still like everybody else. After seeing him jump around for the first hour, Johnson got smart and sent Shaky to work with the house gang.

Shaky pushed the pail along for one of the dudes who was mopping, talking to kids as he passed their beds.

"Don't nobody carry on with him! I want silence!" barked Johnson.

After that, it was just Shaky talking to himself as he walked.

There weren't any clocks in the house you could look at. All of the COs have wristwatches. Inmates can wear watches, too, as long as the bands aren't metal. And a couple of the kids on our side had them. I never wanted one because it only mattered what time the COs said it was. They could make their watches say anything they wanted. Besides, the only time that *really* counts in jail is days.

Brick was going through his bucket, taking inventory. I saw him juggle with guys in the beds next to his. He even had some dude pass smokes off into the next row for him.

For all his tough talk, Brick didn't act like a killer. He acted like a greedy kid that wanted to be somebody.

Maybe he just needed to learn some manners.

Sanchez told me Brick had been in the Sprungs for almost four months, and that he moved in on kids because he'd been locked up before and knew how the game was played. Then he picked doldiers that were too stupid to run the game for themselves.

Brick was already on probation for robbery and couldn't afford to cop out to a new charge. If he did, he'd get even more time for breaking his promise to the state to stay clean after his last case.

"I got a paid lawyer. A good one," I'd heard Brick bragging to dudes. "My grandmother had the money to bail me out. But I said *nahhh*. I can live here, no problem. Take that cheddar and buy me the best mouthpiece there is. There ain't a shred of evidence against me a smart lawyer can't knock down."

Just after lights-out it started to rain. It beat down on top of the bubble like a drum. I ran my fingers over my scar where the skin had gotten tight and hard. You couldn't escape the sound of being inside that drum, nobody could. You could only learn to deal with it.

FRIDAY, JUNE 12

CHAPTER
26

I was awake when the Turtles started across the yard the next morning. I saw them through the windows of the emergency doors in the back of the house and I knew what to expect.

They brought crowbars, dogs, and an X-ray machine. There were at least twenty regular COs behind them. That whole outfit settled in front of Sprung #3 for a minute. Then the Turtles came inside first.

Most of the house was still asleep when the Turtles' captain got on a bullhorn.

"Everybody up!" he ordered. "Stand beside your beds with your fingers locked behind your heads."

"Do it now! Do it now!" hollered one Turtle after another, punching inmates in the kidneys if they didn't move fast enough.

Some kids didn't know what was happening.

I'd got on a pair of pants and sneakers before they even came inside. But most dudes were caught sleeping and had to stand barefoot in their underwear.

The Turtles are always on point, acting like super-COs 24/7. And they're looking for high drama from the word Go.

They get their name from the gear they wear. When there's a riot in the jail, they get dressed in helmets and big chest protectors that cover them from front to back. That way no one can stab them with a banger. When they put everything on, they look just like turtles in their shells.

They wear a darker uniform than the regular COs—one that's almost black, like Darth Vader's. And even when they aren't wearing those shells, kids still call them "Turtles."

Most dudes knew them from the corridors in the main building.

If your house is on the move and Turtles pass your way, inmates have to play the wall and let them go by first. They even make you put your head down, because you're not allowed to look them in the face.

There's always one Turtle that will make a show of it and start to scream at some kid who's hanging on the wall.

"Are you looking at me, maggot? Put your eyes on me again!" he'll warn.

Two or three Turtles will circle around the kid in case he talks back. But the kid just usually shits a brick in his pants. Then everybody goes back to their house talking about how crazy the Turtles are and how nobody in their right mind would ever want to fight them.

The Turtles stood watch inside the house while a search crew of COs went through everybody's stuff.

COs patted down dudes and emptied their buckets onto the floor. Then they flipped the beds over and made everyone drag their mattresses to the X-ray machine. Most of the mattresses were stink-old. They were so ripped you couldn't tell if a dude had buried a weapon in one or not. So they used the machine to make sure.

All the COs wore rubber gloves while they searched. It was like our shit would give them some sort of disease if it touched their skin. The only things I had in my bucket were a couple of shirts and an extra pair of pants. The COs went through them quick and then made me open my mouth and move my tongue around to see if I was hiding any razor blades.

The search team found a homemade banger in Luis's mattress.

"All right, there's number one," said a CO, celebrating.

The COs with the X-ray machine saw it clear as day on their monitor. They dug it out of the stuffing and were waving it around in the air like a prize.

The banger was made from a sharpened piece of metal, with tape wrapped around the bottom for a handle.

"This was ripped off the bottom of a chair," said a CO. "Probably from the school trailer."

"Hey, genius. I'm glad you picked something up in that school," a CO taunted Luis.

The Turtles' captain served Luis with a write-up on the spot and then packed his ass up.

Luis would do sixty days in the bing for sure.

It doesn't matter if a weapon is yours or not. If they even find it *near* your shit, you get charged. Lots of times a dude will slide a banger across the floor, just to get rid of it when things get hot. If it winds up under your bed, you're the one that gets screwed.

The dogs sniffed around for drugs, but didn't find any.

Dawson and Arrigo were watching from up front with Captain Montenez. They didn't show much expression at all. The less the search team found, the better those three were going to look.

Brick was standing at his bed stone-faced. If the house got burned for the banger, it would be because of *his* doldier. I wondered if other dudes would get brave and give him lip for that. He was already weaker with Luis out the door.

The search team even tore through the GED books in the house. They were looking for razors hidden between the pages and in the bindings.

"Officer, I need that book," pleaded a kid who was taking the test soon.

"Stop crying, little boy," ripped a CO. "We do this so nothing happens to you. We don't want anybody getting cut."

Those words stung me hard.

I wanted to scream at the top of my lungs, "Assholes! If you'd checked the kid that cut me coming back from court, I wouldn't look like this! I'd have one less thing to worry about all my life!"

And I would have been satisfied to say it, even while they were beating me senseless. But I knew better.

For all their tearing shit apart, there was still no sign of Murray's chalk holder. It took them an hour and a half to leave the house a total mess. And it took almost two hours of work to put it all back together after they'd gone.

When Montenez left, Dawson and Arrigo broke out in big smiles.

"One banger's not so bad," Arrigo said.

"That's a pretty clean house in anybody's book," bragged Dawson.

Then they told us the captain burned the house from commissary that afternoon because of Luis's banger. But after that, we were clear.

Now maybe Murray was the only one left who still believed we swiped his stupid chalk holder.

CHAPTER
27

hey finally brought us over to the school, and it was almost time for lunch. It should have been the end of Mrs. Daniels's science class, but Demarco was there instead. He knew why we were late and wanted to hear about the search.

"Did they find it?" he asked.

"Nope," answered one kid.

"Told you we didn't have it," said another one.

Dudes started to rank on Murray.

"They should lock his ass up here for lying."

"I'd make him wash my drawers and do the Pogo every night."

"That four-eyed, crooked-nosed bastard."

Demarco wouldn't let us talk like that in front of him. He asked dudes to stop, and they pulled back. But kids were really letting loose about how school was just a place for them to get into more trouble for shit they didn't do.

Then Murray walked in to start his history class. Everybody got quiet, and no one would even look at him. We weren't about to do his work.

I heard him starting to write on the board when Demarco shouted, "What?"

"There it is! He's got it!" yelled Jersey.

Murray was using his damn chalk holder. He was writing on the blackboard with it like nothing had ever happened.

"Where did you find it?" demanded Demarco.

But before Demarco got an answer, he had to hold kids back from stepping hard to Murray. Four or five dudes were already out of their seats and raging.

The COs heard the noise and came busting in.

Kids turned right to them, pointing at Murray and his damn chalk holder, like he was an inmate they were ratting out.

I thought Arrigo was going to flip on him right there in front of us.

"Is that the one that got stolen yesterday?" he hollered.

Murray was trying to get him out of the room to talk, but kids started howling at the top of their lungs. There was so much noise you couldn't make out a thing. Finally, Arrigo just snapped. He pounded his fist on the desk and screamed, "Everybody sit down and shut up!"

Dudes ran for their chairs faster than I'd ever seen—not

because they were scared, but because they were in the right. The game was finally working on their side.

Dawson was in the doorway the whole time taking in the scene. He never said a word. He didn't have to. The look on his face said enough. He was wound up tighter than tight, like his face was going to explode.

"Give me that!" screeched Arrigo, taking the holder away from Murray.

Arrigo was so pissed that he ripped the chalk out and slammed it down on the desk. It splintered into pieces that went shooting across the room.

"Watch the class, Demarco," demanded Arrigo. "And *you*," he said to Murray, "come outside with me."

"I can't," said Murray, smug. "I'm assigned to teach this—"

"This is jail! I'm in charge!" hollered Arrigo. "Now get out in that hall!"

I know the same current that shot through me was buzzing inside of every kid as Murray did the perp walk behind Arrigo.

Dawson was already on the phone calling Montenez, while Arrigo waited for Murray to catch up to him. Kids in every classroom were pressed up against the windows and looking out into the hall, and had their doors cracked open to hear.

Arrigo held the chalk holder out to Murray and said, "Well?"

That's when that high-heeled Ms. Jackson showed up and wanted to know why Arrigo had her teacher out of class.

"Corrections business, Ms. Principal," said Dawson through his teeth. "Maybe you heard, there's jail going on here."

"Look," said Murray. "I found it at the bottom of my bag yesterday in between some papers and—"

"Yesterday!" Arrigo cut in. "When yesterday? While you were still here?"

"I told Ms. Jackson I found it," answered Murray. "She was going to report it to—"

"You knew, too?" Arrigo said, turning to her. "And you didn't come over to the house and tell us?"

"You saw the search squad out in the yard this morning," said Dawson. "You knew the house wasn't coming out for school. What did you think we were looking for?"

"We're not correction officers," snarled the principal.

"That's right, you're not," said Arrigo. "You may have book smarts, lady, but you don't have any real brains. And you think *we're* all stupid? Now we think the same about the teachers!"

Murray started back to class, but Arrigo made him stay.

"This is metal," he said, with the holder flat in his palm. "You're in possession of contraband."

"The captain already made it clear. You shouldn't have this here," said Dawson.

Captain Montenez got to the trailer, and Ms. Jackson tried to say something to him first. But he walked past her and Murray like they didn't exist.

He turned his radio down and asked the COs, "Where is it?"

Arrigo handed the chalk holder to Montenez and said, "These two found it *yesterday*."

The captain told Dawson to call for an escort. Then he turned to Murray and said, "Give me your pass!"

Kids were knocked flat by that. Murray unclipped the plastic card from his shirt and gave it over. Now he was just like us, at the mercy of Corrections. Some dudes whispered that they might even arrest him.

"She knew, too," said Arrigo, pointing to Ms. Jackson.

"*She's* the principal. I can't do anything about her—yet," said Montenez.

Then the captain stared down the two of them and just went off.

"Do you want me to call these kids out into the hall so you can explain to them why they got strip-searched? Or why their house got torn apart this morning? And you had this all along," he steamed, lifting the chalk holder high into the light. "Do you know how much money you cost the city in overtime? They ought to take it out of your paychecks."

Ms. Jackson slipped into the teachers' room during the middle of it all to hide, but Murray stayed put and took it.

"How about if you explain it to these kids yourself?" Montenez asked him.

But Murray just stood there like a dummy and didn't answer.

"At least we turned up a banger out of this whole mess," the captain said to his officers.

The escort came and Montenez told him to take Murray to the front gate.

"Make sure he gets off the Island," he said in a loud voice.

Murray went into the storeroom with the escort to pack his stuff. Then Arrigo called us out for lunch. We deuced it up in the hall and could see Murray putting his books into a cardboard box. Dudes wanted to snap on him so bad, but Montenez was wearing a grill to kill.

"Remember, you're still inmates here," the captain said, looking us over.

We were lined up outside the mess hall when the escort took Murray across the yard. He was carrying the cardboard box with both hands and had a briefcase stuck under his arm. He had to pass right by us to get to the gate, and dudes' eyes just lit up.

"Say one thing to him while the captain's still here and I'll burn this house forever," warned Arrigo.

Murray never even raised his sorry head to look at us as he passed. But we watched him until he disappeared around the corner.

CHAPTER 28

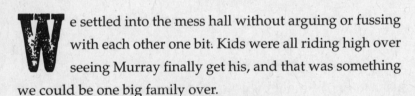

We settled into the mess hall without arguing or fussing with each other one bit. Kids were all riding high over seeing Murray finally get his, and that was something we could be one big family over.

Jail food never tasted any better to me.

We had chili over white rice, and the mess hall workers piled bread high on our trays. It was like a celebration, or as close as you could get to one on Rikers Island without everybody beating their cases at the same time.

As soon as we got back to the house after school, kids were trying to run the sympathy routine on Dawson and Arrigo.

"Look at how that rat Murray did us dirty."

"A strip search, the Turtles—damn, we deserve somethin'."

"Yeah, come on, bless us."

None of it got us to commissary.

"Yeah, how'd that banger get here?" asked Dawson. "The Tooth Fairy?"

If Ms. Armstrong was on duty we might have had a shot. Maybe she would have gotten on the phone and tried to talk to Montenez. Still, dudes had to try and run that routine before Officer Johnson came on. Johnson would have listened for about five seconds before he started smacking kids around for trying to play him.

Brick was quiet about the whole thing. I guess he knew that some of this was going to get kicked back his way. Why should kids sweat not being able to pay him now? It was his doldier that got them burned. Besides, Luis had kept tabs on how much all the Spanish dudes in the house owed. Brick didn't even know their names.

He told Sanchez to straighten it all out for him. Brick said he'd wipe out what Sanchez owed if he represented him with the Spanish kids. But Sanchez had already copped out to his drug charge in court and only figured to be around for a couple more days. As soon as a bed popped open up north, he'd be on the first bus off Rikers Island. Those Spanish kids knew that and wouldn't fess up to him about who owed what.

Barnett couldn't get it done because he didn't speak their language, and those guys would just pretend that they didn't understand any English.

I understood why Sanchez wanted to settle his account so bad before he left.

"If I'm going stay in the system, I don't want a reputation

like that hanging over my head," Sanchez had told me. "I don't need it to pop back up at the wrong time. All it takes is for one dude from the house to follow me up north and spread the word. Then what if somebody claims to know Brick and wants to collect for him? It happens to kids in the houses down here all the time. It could be ten times worse up there with adults pulling the strings."

No one needed to feel sorry about Brick getting short-changed. Sanchez said that Brick had his grandmother under heavy pressure. She put money into his account every month, and that kept his store fat and healthy.

Anyway, he still had plenty of shit to juggle in his bucket. Until next Friday, he was the only store around and his prices just went up. It was three-for-one now. But kids were hungry and needed to smoke.

Since the house was on the burn, Barnett called it a "fire sale." Shaky was even going around screaming like a siren as he made deliveries. He'd speed around the house in an invisible fire engine. Then he'd throw on the brakes in front of some kid's bed and juggle for Brick.

Brick wouldn't deal to the Spanish dudes anymore. He couldn't keep track of them, and they'd already beat him for most of what they owed.

"You represent me in the time you got left here," Brick told Sanchez. "You're my go-between with those guys. They'll cave soon. And I'll let you know how much of your tab you've worked off by the results."

I knew that something in the house had to give. Those Spanish dudes had decent numbers on the north side and the south. Once they saw that Brick was losing his grip and had nothing to offer, there was no reason for them to play his game anymore.

That night, they just stepped to the phones during prime time and started to dial. They tied up the lines and watched each other's backs while they were talking.

Other kids were busy peeping in on the action, but Brick stayed cool.

"Be the cash register and keep track of it all," he told Sanchez, who stood there with a pad and pencil.

Brick tried his best to make it look like he'd charge them later.

But he was just playing the middle now and hoping the black kids wouldn't catch on. Then he would really be out of business.

Long after lights-out, I could hear those Spanish dudes whispering in their language. Sometimes they'd just laugh. And deep down, I was laughing with them.

SATURDAY, JUNE 13

CHAPTER
29

During rec the next day, most of the house was just lying out on the bleachers. It was hot and the heat was coming up off the concrete. There were just enough players for one basketball game. Ritz was playing on the main court with the good ball for a change. His team had won three games in a row, and he was showing off all his skills. Kids from the bleachers started calling him "Crackerjack." And every time he scored or passed the ball to somebody cutting wide-open to the hoop, they'd scream out his new tag.

Some dudes started saying that Ritz was even better than big Barnett. Then Brick got to the yard and started ranking on kids for thinking like that.

"No white boy runs anything out here," he laughed. "This is the hood, not some Wall Street."

But kids were willing to back Ritz against Brick's doldier.

"I'll lay two-to-one on my boy for all you fools," spouted Brick.

They got Barnett out of the dayroom and even stopped a game right in the middle just to get those two on the court alone. It was "Crackerjack" against "Chocolate Thunder." Everybody made their bets, and the kids who'd backed Ritz promised him a piece of the action if he won.

Only Ritz didn't need the idea of winning money to get hyped. Just proving he was somebody in that house would keep him going hard.

"This is gonna be for every insult I ever took in this place," he said, focused.

Barnett wanted to warm up and missed a couple of shots from the outside. Then he pounded the rock on the floor, making a few layups.

"Bring it on, white boy," Barnett growled.

The game was Straight Eleven.

Ritz dribbled between his legs and blew by Barnett with his right hand to score first. Then he faked right and spun left for another easy basket.

Before long it was 5–0, and Barnett hadn't even touched the rock yet.

The next time Ritz went to the hoop, Barnett leveled him. He laid him out flat with a shoulder, then picked up the ball and scored.

Ritz was sitting on his ass, listening to dudes roar.

"Told you he'd bounce more than the ball!"

"Get up, Crackerjack. I got a week's worth of cookies riding on you!"

Ritz had no beef about getting bounced.

The rules for jailhouse ball are simple: no blood, no foul.

The big man couldn't hit a shot, and Ritz kept making him pick up his dribble twenty feet from the basket. But Barnett was pounding him senseless. So Ritz had to throw up thirty-footers just to get a clean shot off.

After almost twenty minutes, the score was still only 7–1.

Sprung #2 was lined up at the door to their house waiting for the yard. But all the rec officers were busy watching the game. They held Sprung #2 up as long as they could, then they finally blew the whistle and took the ball.

Everyone who'd bet on Ritz wanted to collect. Most dudes that backed Barnett paid off. The big man even nodded his head to Ritz on the way off the court. But Brick claimed the game wasn't official.

"Your man didn't get to eleven, did he?" Brick argued. "Game called."

Brick was just being ass-stupid. He could have paid everybody and got it all back on the juggle. Now even more kids were just going to hold a grudge against him.

It was almost four o'clock when a CO screamed, "Forty, visit!"

I was supposed to be going home in six days, if the system didn't find a new way to screw me. And that was a worry I'd been carrying around inside of me like a two-ton weight.

When it started getting late, I thought Mom might skip this visit, trying not to jinx anything in court. But there she was for me.

The escort had already picked up kids from Sprung #1 and #2. Most of them walked across the yard like they were somebody. Some were fronting. Others were serious about their reps. I walked out of Sprung #3 and the only thing those kids saw was the cut on my face. I was either a killer or a herb to them, nothing more.

We hit the main building, stopping at the mods along the way for more inmates.

I started to run it over in my brain, what I'd do if we ever picked up the kid who'd cut me—if that spiderweb on his neck was within my reach. I wouldn't say a thing. I'd just rush him. I'd put two hands around his throat and ram his head against the gate before the COs could stop me.

We hit almost every mod in the building, and I just got deeper into that scene at every door. I'd watch each dude's face as he stepped into the hall, with my eyes running down to his neck.

My heart was beating hard.

I was ready to be an animal and put it all straight.

But there was no one to aim it at.

We got to the visit floor and I was raging inside. I was staring up at the ceiling trying to slow down and breathe normal again.

That's when you find trouble in jail. You're all pumped up

over something. Then somebody says shit to you. It's easy to fight the wrong dude just because he's standing there.

"You know the drill, kid," a CO told me. "I need to see you the way your mama brought you into this world."

I took off my clothes. Then he made me lift up my arms and spread my butt cheeks.

"You pass," he said, moving on to the next inmate.

I put on the orange jumper and slippers, waiting to get called.

This time Mom would see me without the bandages on my face. And I was hoping it wouldn't make her feel too bad.

They finally called me out onto the floor, and I was walking with my head down behind the CO. I looked up all at once and thought I was at the wrong table because of all the faces. Mom had brought Grandma and my sisters with her. And I almost couldn't believe they were really there.

Suddenly, all that anger was gone and a thousand fears flashed through my brain about how they'd react.

I knew Mom wouldn't bring them without telling about my cut first.

Trisha and Tina ran up to hug me, like it was nothing. I closed my eyes and could hear their good shoes tapping on the floor.

I leaned down to kiss Grandma, and she said my name.

Mom stood up and touched my face.

"This is what it is," she said, and they all looked.

I studied them, too. My sisters had gotten bigger, and

Grandma was a little older. Then I focused on Mom's face to make sure she was all right.

She looked stronger than I'd ever seen her before.

"This is the only time I'm ever coming to jail, and that's because I love you, child!" Grandma said.

Before I could say anything, Mom answered, "You won't *ever* have to come back, Mama. The next time we're all together, it'll be at home."

"Amen," said Grandma.

Mom told her, "Martin's been going to school here."

"This is where too many of our boys go back to school," Grandma said, looking around the visit floor.

Mom just nodded her head, holding my sisters tight by their hands.

But I didn't want to talk about the damn system. I wouldn't waste my breath on that now. I didn't want to ruin this good feeling with them all there.

I knew that I missed being with my family. But I didn't understand how much until we were all in one place again. It didn't matter that we were on Rikers Island. It didn't matter that we were at a plastic table or that I was wearing an orange jumpsuit. It didn't even matter that I had this cut on my face.

That night in the Sprung, I looked around and didn't see anything I would miss when I left. And the only house I ever wanted to be in again was my own.

SUNDAY, JUNE 14

CHAPTER
30

I knew something was going on when I woke up. The COs from the night before were still on duty. Then one of the kids asked about going to church service.

"You're lucky God's everywhere 'cause the Island's on total lockdown," the CO said. "There's no movement."

A couple of dudes were standing by the big window at the back of the house. That's when I noticed the Turtles dressed up in their gear walking along the outside of the double fences and down by the water.

Then the COs woke everybody up and took the count twice with kids standing at their beds.

"Somewhere on the Island the count has to be off," Sanchez whispered. "There's an inmate missing for sure."

This was the second time it had happened since I'd been locked up.

The Department of Corrections calls it a "red alert." They close the bridge and won't let anyone off the Island. The last tour of COs has to stay at their posts, and the new ones coming on do all the searching.

Inmates can't go anywhere. There's no mess hall, no law library, no rec, and no visits. Everybody just sits around and gets tight.

The last time, they searched for five or six hours until the warden decided that inmate was long gone. It put a smile on dudes' faces to think that you could really bust out and maybe beat the game. But a week later, we saw in the newspaper that the NYPD nabbed him. They caught him hiding at his girl's crib in Queens Village. He was sound asleep and the cops just walked in and cuffed him.

Most kids thought that dude was stupid for staying with his girl. She probably visited him before, and Corrections knew her address from the sign-in book. Still, it took them a week to catch his ass. He could have got what he wanted from her on the first night and then split. That guy was smart enough to escape, but dumb in other ways.

"They can add seven years to your sentence for busting out," said Jersey. "How you gonna beat that rap?"

"Yeah, what can you say? 'It wasn't me you found outside the gates,'" mocked Ritz.

Corrections wouldn't tell anyone how that last guy escaped. Maybe he even got a deal to keep his mouth shut about how he'd done it.

No matter what anybody says, the best way off of Rikers

Island is through the front gate. Kids are always scoping the passes that civilians wear. The teachers in the Sprungs keep them clipped to their shirts, and sometimes they drop. If a kid got a hold of one and had the right kind of clothes, he could just walk out with the crowd.

A teacher like Mr. Rowe was so old and stupid that you could walk right up to him in the parking lot and say you just got paroled. He'd probably give you a ride over the bridge and maybe even to your front door. Then the next day the FBI would be all over his ass.

But there are other ways off Rikers, too.

Every dude I ever met on the Island thought he could swim the half mile to LaGuardia Airport.

Some kids started wondering if the guy who was missing swam for it.

· "The water looks all calm, but I hear there's wicked currents," said Jersey.

"Corrections has a boat that passes by on the regular, too," Ritz said. "I see it all the time."

I'd never even heard of anybody who made it into the water. And I don't know what kind of chance you'd have with the police at the airport if you got across. When they see you streaking across the runway soaking wet, they might catch on faster than you think.

You could tell from the Turtles' faces that they were nervous. I never thought I'd see a squad of COs with clubs and helmets look spooked, but they were.

"That's because they know if a dude could bust out, he

could get his hands on a gun," Sanchez told me. "Then all their padding wouldn't mean shit."

Most COs carry guns with them out in the world. If they run across a dude they smacked around on the Island it could be drama. There wouldn't be a whole squad to back them up either. It would just be one on one, and that tin badge wouldn't count for much.

Most of the COs I had on the Island were square with me. And if I saw most of them out in the world, I'd just walk past without saying anything. But if I ever saw Officer Johnson on a street corner, I'd probably be scared shitless and run.

By two o'clock there were more kids looking out the back window than watching TV in the dayroom.

Then a CO announced, "Alarm's over. Lunch will be late, but it's coming."

The COs wouldn't say anything about who was missing or what happened. Corrections tries to keep you in the dark so you don't get any big ideas of your own.

They brought the food out from the main building, with the mess hall workers moving double-time. When we finally got lunch it was past three o'clock. Not everybody could afford Brick's new prices to juggle. Most kids were light in their buckets and didn't eat since supper the night before, including me.

We got served cheese sandwiches.

"How old's this cheese? It's hard and brown around the corners," some dude complained.

But kids were practically starving and wolfed those sand-wiches down like it was McDonald's.

We marched back to the house from the mess hall, and Ms. Armstrong was sitting up front giving out mail. I was surprised when she put a letter in my hand. Usually my sisters sent me cards they made in grade school with flowers pasted on them. But this envelope was flat and thin.

The address in the corner read, "Auburn Correctional Facility." The letter was from my pops and postmarked June 4th, two days after I'd got cut.

It was the first time I'd heard from him since I'd been locked up. And I wasn't sure if I was ready for what he would say.

There was a knot inside me that kept getting tighter, so I put the letter down on my bed and walked in circles around the house.

Finally, I just grabbed for it.

I opened it and tried to read fast. But I got stuck halfway through the first sentence, and the same words kept running over in my head.

"Son, let me tell you something about jail. . . . Son, let me tell you something . . . let me tell you something about jail. . . ."

I climbed into bed, fell back on the pillow, and pushed the letter up over my face. The lights from the top of the house kept coming through the paper, and I had to hold it off to the side to see clearly.

I took a deep breath and started from the beginning.

Son, let me tell you something about jail
because its the only thing I ever learned good,
and I want you to learn more then me in this
life, they have traps to keep you here, you have
to look down every day to see it, they put big
holes in the floor, every day they put it some
place new, inmates and C.O. dig holes together,
they dont want you to be happy or ever go
home again, that way the C.O. can keep their
good job, your old enough to understand what
I say, they want to steal you from your family
to keep them poor in the dirt, dont let them do
it to you, keep your foot out of the traps, keep
your eyes looking down for the holes, go home
and help your mother, and watch your sisters
for me.

Love, Pops
xxxxxooo

That was the first time I'd ever heard him talk about jail.
Two or three times a year, Mom would take me with her to
visit him. He would always ask how I was doing in school
and if I was staying out of trouble. He never talked about any
problems or if it was rough for him there. But things were different now. I could understand where he was coming from,
and he could be straight with me. It felt bad to think about it,
but being locked up was something we shared together.

I kissed his letter and put it in my pocket so I wouldn't lose it.

That night Sanchez said Brick wanted to meet with Jersey, Ritz, and me. I didn't want to have anything to do with it, but Jersey and Ritz wanted to hear him out.

"I'll bet you he begs for our help," said Jersey, pumped up.

"That's something I gotta see," Ritz said. "I can't risk missing that."

When I couldn't talk them out of it, I decided to go along so they wouldn't get into anything stupid. But I was curious, too.

Brick got us in the corner of the dayroom and talked like it was nothing special. He said we could live in the house for free. We could eat and smoke from his store and use the phones, like it was all ours. All we had to do was play on his side and back him up to the end.

When we didn't jump at his offer right away, he started to yap.

"You dudes don't know when you've got it good," he said. "See what happens if I close up shop and kids are sparring over every little thing. This house will get burned every other—"

"We've got to think it over," Jersey cut him off, before walking away.

I almost fell back.

Jersey had laid it on Brick right to his face.

I knew he was pissed at being replaced by Shaky. Dudes in the house had even started calling him "less than a retard."

But Jersey had got some real fire in his belly since then, and Brick's rep had cooled way down.

After Brick left, Ritz had a big shit-eating grin on his face.

"I want to be the one to tell Brick no," Ritz said. "Tomorrow. Let's make him sweat it overnight."

It was hard to believe, but the only white boy in the Sprungs was going to tell the house gangster that he wouldn't watch his back.

"How can you turn that sweet deal down?" asked Sanchez, upset as anything when I told him how it went down.

I felt bad for Sanchez, who had to front for Brick.

He was an all-right dude. But that's what happens when you get in deep and owe somebody. Sometimes you have to play the wrong side.

It was almost lights-out.

I climbed into bed, careful, still looking for the traps and holes.

MONDAY,
JUNE 15

CHAPTER
31

In school, Demarco wouldn't even crack a smile over Murray getting tossed off the Island. Kids pushed him to say that he was happy about it. Only he wouldn't go there.

"My lesson today's too important to waste time on *him*," said Demarco. "It starts off like this: Where do you want to be in five years?"

Demarco did tell us that Murray wasn't really fired. He was sitting in a Board of Education office somewhere in Queens, until everything got looked into. And he'd probably just get sent to another school in the end.

"It sounds like the pen for teachers," cracked Jersey.

"In fact, Murray's collecting the same money, even though he's not teaching," said Demarco.

"That's probably why he did it," some dude said. "A paid vacation."

And nobody argued.

After a while, most kids were headfirst into writing an answer to Demarco's question. But I was stuck. I didn't know where I wanted to be in five years, except home.

"If you can't find the exact place," Demarco told me, "then write about what it should be like there."

I wrote that I wanted to be in a place where people know my real name, a place where I could find something important to do with my life. That there should always be at least one other person around who cares about me, and maybe someone extra special to watch out for the traps and fill in all the holes.

Demarco looked at it and said he liked it fine, but didn't understand the part about the traps and holes. So I showed him Pops's letter and let him read it.

"Your father must really love you to want to share what he's learned," said Demarco, when he'd finished. "Martin, you should be proud to have this kind of relationship with him."

Other dudes wanted to see the letter, too, but I wouldn't let them. I said it was private, and that Demarco was the teacher and couldn't understand my answer without reading it.

I guess I really wanted Demarco to see it from the start. I knew it was full of mistakes and bad spelling, but I didn't care. I wanted him to say something good, like Pops was *somebody*.

And he did.

Just as Demarco's time was up, Mr. Green, the guidance counselor, came to the door and called Sanchez outside again. Since he'd started seeing Green, Sanchez seemed braver about going upstate. Or maybe he just didn't have the time to worry about it since Brick kept him hopping now.

I never asked Sanchez what he talked about with the counselor, and he never said anything about it either.

There are no bells to signal when a class is over in the Sprungs. The only bells that go off in jail are alarms, and the COs wouldn't want to mix up the two. So teachers go to the door of their next class when it's time, keeping one eye on the kids they left behind. It hardly ever goes smooth with five teachers trying to pull off that trick at the same time.

A dude from another room snuck over to us while the teachers were changing. He flashed a piece of carbon paper, and dudes picked their heads up like he had the key to the front gate.

"I got it from Murray's substitute, Mr. Powell," the dude said.

"He a herb?" somebody asked.

"Can't tell yet," he answered. "But he's at least stupid-new."

Right away kids started to scheme. A new teacher meant someone who didn't know the system and maybe somebody you could play big-time.

Then Miss Archer arrived and gave that dude the boot from our room.

"Let's go," she said, tugging him by the arm all the way to the door.

He just smiled and rolled his eyes at her.

"You can touch me anytime you want," he said. "I love you."

Inmates use carbon paper to make jailhouse tattoos. First, you heat a safety pin over a match to kill all the germs. Then you use the ink on the paper to fill in the holes you leave with the pin on a dude's arm. Some kids are good at it. Other tattoos look like shit and you can't even figure them out.

I was always too scared of the pain to get one, in jail or out in the world. But I'd laugh at that pinprick now. I was stuck with a different kind of mark. One I couldn't cover up.

The COs won't let you have carbon paper. They don't give a damn about tattoos. They think you'll use it to print a fake ID. Tinfoil is contraband, too. They're afraid you'll try to copy a badge and walk out.

Miss Archer had us writing about the grades we deserved in her math class. She even made kids read the assignment out loud. Most of them started out with, "I never disrespected you," or, "Everybody knows how you feel about me." Dudes were really loving it, but I didn't know what to write because I'd only been in her class for a week.

I glanced out the big window into the hall. I saw Ms. Jackson with Captain Montenez and a full-bird deputy warden watching us.

Jersey saw them, too.

"Oh, shit. Deputy warden on deck," he said, without ever moving his lips.

Dudes just froze and only their eyes turned sideways to

see, because that deputy warden had probably ten times the power of a captain.

After a while, they all moved on to the classroom across the way.

Everything was quiet for a second, then Montenez screamed for the COs.

I could see him charge into Mrs. Daniels's room and snatch up a kid who was sleeping. That kid probably got yanked out of some good dream to find himself hooked under the neck by Montenez and being dragged through the hall.

"Not in my school you don't!" hollered Montenez, shoving the kid into the officers' desk. "Mr. Arrigo, pack this young man up. We'll see if he likes sleeping in the building with all the wolves running around."

The deputy warden nodded his head in approval. And it was plain to see that since the COs and teachers weren't going to hammer kids about sleeping, that miserable Ms. Jackson had gone and found herself a deputy warden that would make them.

Mrs. Daniels ran into the hall and started arguing with Montenez.

"You can't put your hands on these kids for no reason!" she yelled. "That's police brutality, and I'll report it!"

Montenez tried to blow her off, but Mrs. Daniels said she was going to write it up and send it to the newspapers.

"These are inmates," the principal told her. "You have to respect the system."

Mrs. Daniels didn't back off, and she wrote down the badge numbers of Montenez and the deputy warden.

By the time things got calmer, Miss Archer was at the door, ready to leave, and Mrs. Daniels was coming into our class.

"I'm going to put something about the solar system up on the board," Mrs. Daniels told us. "Copy it down and give me quiet so I can write something."

When she was done at the board, Mrs. Daniels pulled out a sheet of paper and put the date up at the top. Dudes crowded around her desk as she wrote how Montenez snatched the kid up, and that he was only sleeping. She wrote how the deputy warden was there and that Ms. Jackson didn't report an assault on a student.

"Damn," Jersey said, amazed. "She's going after Montenez in his own jail."

"It's not *his* jail. He doesn't own *it* or *you*," Mrs. Daniels said.

One of the house snitches went right to Dawson and Arrigo with the news.

They were steamed and tried to talk Mrs. Daniels out of it, but she wouldn't listen.

Then Carter came in and said, "I'm sorry to say this, but maybe we should stop watching your back, Mrs. D."

Mrs. Daniels wrote that down, too, and called it a threat.

The truth was that the COs *didn't* need to watch her back anymore. Kids gave her mad props for what she was doing. Mrs. Daniels was putting herself out there for us like nobody had before. Right then, dudes would have done anything for her. She was free and clear with us.

We had almost forgot about Murray's substitute, until he showed up at our door once science class was over. He had a Caribbean accent and was wearing a suit and tie, with a history book under his arm. Kids walked him into class, pulled out his chair, and sat his fresh ass down.

We started asking him questions about his family, the kind of car he drove, and where he lived. After a few minutes, we knew lots of things about Mr. Powell, like that he lived on State Street in Brooklyn. And his eyes even lit up when dudes started calling him "Pow."

Then kids noticed the cell phone on his belt.

"Hey, Pow, that's off the hook. Let me have a look at that," a dude said.

"I'd rather just hold onto it," said Powell.

Before you knew it, the dude told him a sob story about not being able to get a hold of his lawyer and Powell gave him the phone.

Then kids were making calls in the corner of the room.

Powell looked like he was starting to get nervous, but he probably didn't know to get the COs.

Dudes argued over who'd use the cell next.

Carter heard the racket from the officers' desk. He busted in and took the phone away. Then Dawson and Arrigo strolled in, laughing their asses off. They gave Powell a big speech right in front of everybody.

"Listen, Mr. Powell," said Arrigo. "I know you're a smart guy and all because you went to college and graduated. But these kids are inmates. Don't give them your watch so they can see the time. They don't need to borrow lunch money. And most of all, don't give out any personal information about yourself."

"Not unless you want them visiting you out in the world," grinned Dawson.

After they left, Powell just looked at us for a while without saying a word.

He was probably feeling like a real jackass.

"Don't worry 'bout it, Pow," said Jersey. "That's the game out here. We've got to test you."

Some dude asked him why he came to teach in jail, and if he was afraid we'd all jump him. That's when the COs called us out for lunch. We just left Powell sitting there before he could answer.

After lunch, we had Mr. Rowe's life skills class. I was the first one back to the room, and he was already there, sitting behind the desk. He looked at me like he'd never seen me before.

"Are you sure this is your class?" he asked.

I couldn't believe it. I'd been sitting five feet from Rowe for a week, with a big cut on my face. But he still had no clue I was his student. He should have been a detective instead of a teacher. Then maybe the jail would be empty and some high school out in the world would be full of kids.

All through class, I kept staring at the yellow pass clipped to Rowe's shirt collar. That plastic ID was the only thing that made him different from me. It was even more important than the color of his white skin. It got him through the gates and home every night without a second look from the COs.

Dudes were screwing around while Rowe was *teaching* us.

Then Brick walked in and called out his name.

"Mr. Roooowe," he said, dragging it out. "Gimme some skin."

But when Rowe reached out to slap his hand, Brick pulled it back and left him hanging there like Super Herb.

The whole class busted out laughing.

Brick took the chair right behind me and Sanchez.

"So what's it gonna be?" he asked in a low voice.

I looked over at Ritz, knowing he'd already delivered the news.

"I don't care what the white boy told me," said Brick. "I'm talking to *you* now."

"I'm straight," I answered. "I don't need anything better."

Brick studied my eyes and said, "You must be going home if you can stay living like this. What are you facing, Forty?"

I wouldn't tell him shit.

I hadn't told anyone in the house about my case, except that it was a drug charge. Soon as dudes find out what you're facing, they can start to play you. Nobody knew I was supposed to be going home on Friday, and it was going to stay that way.

Brick picked up, annoyed now, and moved to the door.

"There should be more new jacks in the house this week. I'll bet some of them will be hungry to play on my team," Brick said, and left.

Sanchez had a worried look on his face. I could see that he had a lot on his mind, so I asked him about it after school.

"Mr. Green checked with the Department of Corrections," answered Sanchez. "He found out that beds are opening soon upstate. He says I should be gone by Thursday morning, the latest."

Then Sanchez talked about holding his own up north and staying clear of trouble. His voice was steady, and it sounded like he believed every word of it. But Sanchez's hands were shaking a little, and I decided to keep a close eye on him for the rest of the day.

That night, Brick called some herb that owed him out of the dayroom. It was a big production. Barnett watched the bathroom door and Brick went inside with the kid. He smacked him around pretty good and the kid walked out all lumped up.

Then Shaky went around telling everyone in the house that Brick was getting serious. I guess that was the good part about having someone like him in your crew. He could get the word out fast. And kids would believe it was just *Shaky being Shaky*—that he couldn't help but say what was in his head, and that he wasn't fronting for you.

TUESDAY, JUNE 16

CHAPTER
32

We got to the school trailer the next morning and everything was set up different. The teachers and the principal were waiting in the hallway, and there was a table with cookies and soda in the corner. Kids saw that and got all excited like they were back in the third grade or something.

Then Ms. Jackson made a speech.

"You're all getting report cards today," she said. "There's going to be a party instead of school because the *teachers* thought you deserved one and *I* approved it. So enjoy."

The sight of all that food had kids biting back calling her Ms. Jerk-off.

"It's all too good for you baby thugs," said Officer Carter.

Mrs. Daniels shot him a harsh look. Then she told us about the different things to do. There were classrooms set up for movies, games, letter writing, reading, and computers.

Most dudes made tracks for the movie room without even knowing what the teachers were going to show. But I waited to see where Demarco was headed and followed him into our classroom where all the games were laid out.

Kids had already pushed seats together and were shuffling dominoes. The COs won't let you play dominoes in the house. Dudes slam them down on the table when they have a good hand, making all kinds of noise. They bet on the games, and somebody's always pissed off at getting stiffed.

Demarco sat behind a chessboard.

"I'll wait for somebody who can play or wants to learn," he said.

I was good at checkers, but I didn't know anything about chess.

"What are the rules?" I asked him.

Demarco was showing me how all the different pieces moved when Sanchez started picking up the black ones and laying them out on the board.

Then the two of them started to play.

I was happy to just watch and try to figure it out.

Shaky was in the room playing Monopoly with another kid. They were flashing the fake money around and acting like they were on the street, making a big drug buy.

"My name's Tony Mon-tan-a," said Shaky, hitting each syllable hard. "I need two keys. Here's my cash you fuck-ing nobody."

Demarco said those two must really like living on Rikers Island and want to come back real soon.

"You need to put more thought into who your heroes are," he scolded them.

They both got quiet for a while. Then they set up the houses and hotels on the properties, calling them their "crack parlors."

Demarco just shook his head.

There were more white pieces off the chessboard than black ones, and Sanchez had Demarco's king on the run. They would both check out the board for a long time before they did anything. Then Demarco made one quick move and Sanchez dropped his face into his hands as the white horse snatched the black queen up.

"Chess is just like jail," Demarco said, winking at me. "You've got to look out for the traps and holes."

It felt good that he remembered what Pops had said.

After that move, Sanchez didn't have any heart left and just stopped trying.

Jersey came in from the movie room and said they were showing *Cool Hand Luke.*

"You gotta check it out," said Jersey. "It's a movie about white guys in jail. Ritz is sitting in the front row and dudes are ranking on him, saying, 'How you like seein' *your* people locked up for a change?'"

Shaky found the "Get Out of Jail Free" card from the Monopoly game and started bouncing around the room with it like he'd just won the lottery.

"I'm free! I'm free!" he shouted. "Everybody, I'm going home!"

Dudes winked at each other and looked at the card like it was for real. They told Shaky to bring it to Captain Montenez and he'd probably walk him out to the front gate.

"I'm not that stupid," he said.

But Shaky went out in the hallway and showed it to the COs.

Carter kicked him straight in the ass and everybody just rolled.

"That's contraband," Carter said. "Consider it confiscated."

Dawson and Arrigo said they would give the card to some kid they liked better, and Shaky got all upset. He bitched about losing the card all day and said he should have sold it to some herb instead.

When we got back from the mess hall, the teachers were in their homerooms. Demarco was holding a stack of legitimate New York City report cards. Dudes were all wound up just to see them in his hand and started to rush Demarco at the desk. He had to scream at kids for real to sit back down.

One dude saw Jersey's card at the top and started calling off his grades. "You got a 90 from Archer and Daniels, 85 from Demarco, and 70 from Rowe," the dude said.

Jersey put his hand out and said, "My props, please."

Demarco quit on getting us to relax and began distributing the cards.

Even kids who never did anything in school and said it was all just total bullshit were grabbing for their report cards. And every time Demarco gave one out, some dude was either bragging about his grades or bitching about how the teachers screwed him.

Sanchez got all 90s, except for Rowe's class.

"Take some college classes after you get settled upstate," Demarco told him.

"I think I've learned enough on Rikers Island," said Sanchez. "Maybe I don't need to know any more."

"These are still just jail report cards, right?" asked Ritz. "They don't even have the name of a real school on them. They just say, 'New York City Department of Education.'"

Demarco stopped handing out the cards and made everybody sit down. When kids saw how serious he was everybody got quiet and waited for him to talk.

"Let me explain something," he said. "These grades are probably the most important ones you'll ever receive. They prove that no matter how tough things get in your life you can still concentrate on school and move ahead. You should really be proud of these report cards. I want you to know that I'm proud to hand them out."

Dudes couldn't help but feel better about themselves after a speech like that.

Me and Ritz were the only ones who didn't get one. We were in class for just six days, and that wasn't enough time to get any real credits. But Demarco had a surprise for us. He'd printed up his own report cards on his computer at home and had the other teachers fill in grades.

"It's just a progress report," he said. "But you can see how you're doing in the classes and send it home to your family."

I got a 90 from Demarco, 85s from Miss Archer and Mrs. Daniels, and a 70 from Mr. Rowe. Soon, kids started to realize that everybody got a 70 from Mr. Rowe.

"That stooge Rowe gave us all the same grade," a kid complained.

That was probably because Rowe didn't know a single student's name. But at least everybody passed, so it wasn't that big a deal.

Only Murray's section was blank. It was the same with all the report cards. No one in the house got a grade for Murray's history class.

Most dudes were boiling mad because of all the shit he'd put them through. Demarco said that he'd even called Murray at his house and asked him for the grades.

"He's so spiteful he won't do a thing till the investigation gets settled," said Demarco. "I spoke to the principal about it this morning, but she couldn't do anything yet. She says she'll look into it."

Then Demarco crossed his fingers with his eyes up to heaven.

That skinny dude Jessup was really pissed off. He was a senior at Roosevelt High School when he got locked up and only needed a history class to graduate. He'd pulled on Murray's dick like a good little boy for months and wanted to get hit off with his credit.

"So when I get out of here, I'll have to go to night school because of that asshole prick," Jessup fumed.

Ms. Jackson was walking through the trailer and Demarco called her inside. Jessup explained his problem to her as respectful as he could. She kept a hand glued to her chin the whole time he was talking, like it was important to think on it.

Then other dudes piped in. They wanted grades for Murray's class, too, and she started to get all fussy.

"There are lots of problems at the end of a semester," she said, moving backward. "And I only have so much time to fix them, but—"

"All we've got around here is time," a dude said.

After that, it was on. Somebody called her "Ms. Jerk-off," and kids started stamping their feet and singing out loud.

"Who you gonna call? Ms. Jerk-off!"

"Who you gonna call? Ms. Jerk-off!"

Demarco never tried to shush them, and stood there next to her like he was bulletproof.

Ms. Jackson stormed out of the room.

"What is this, music class now, Mr. Costa?" asked Arrigo, as he got to the door.

When he found out what happened, Arrigo made Jessup knock on the principal's door with his toothpick arms and warned him to be nice.

"Please, Ms. Jackson. I need this credit to graduate," said Jessup.

But she was writing away and wouldn't get out of her chair.

Then Dawson knocked and asked her to come outside.

"When you ask these kids to buy into your program and

not act like junior thugs, you've got to give them what you promised," Dawson said to her in the hall, with plenty of us listening in. "Now, can you help this young man?"

"I'm not about to work with inmates who are threatening and abusive to me," she answered.

"I didn't say anything disrespectful to you," Jessup said. "That was the rest of them, not me!"

"You were the leader," she said, pointing a finger at him.

He took a fast step forward and screeched, "The leader?"

Arrigo got in front of Jessup, pushing him back.

"And I'm going to write it up that way, too," Ms. Jackson warned.

That's when Jessup snapped, "Who are you going to write up? Me?"

Now Arrigo was holding him back with one hand, and he gave Jessup a good shove back inside a classroom. But Jessup stopped short and balled up his fist.

Arrigo's eyes lit up.

He punched Jessup in the face like he was fighting Mike Tyson.

Jessup's head hit the side of a door before he bounced to the floor. That's how fast things can change on Rikers.

Arrigo was standing over him, screaming, "Don't you ever make a fist to me again! I could have fuckin' killed you, kid!"

"I'm not going to stand for this anymore!" yelled Mrs. Daniels, charging through the hall.

She passed everyone and headed straight for the trailer door. Maybe she was going home, or to the Department of

Education, or to the newspapers. Nobody really knew for sure. But she was out of there. And she looked like somebody who wanted to settle a score.

"How about just saying, 'Thank you for protecting me all this time!'" Arrigo called after her.

Carter pulled Jessup off the floor and threw him on the wall. Jessup's eye was already swollen shut and the side of his face was cut from where he'd hit the door.

"Look at you, asshole. Now we've got to send you to the clinic and write this shit up," blasted Arrigo.

"Never mind him, look at you," said Dawson.

"I know, too clean. It's gotta be my fault then," Arrigo said.

Then Arrigo disappeared around the corner for a minute and came back with a shiner of his own. I couldn't believe it. That sick bastard punched himself in the eye. He pounded on his own face until his eye swelled up good. Now it would look like he had a good reason for pounding that toothpick of a kid.

"Well, how does it look?" he asked.

"It'll do. But we'll need witness statements," Dawson answered.

"Look what you did to my partner, kid," said Carter, like he almost believed it. "That's an attack on staff."

Only Jessup was too beat down to even answer.

Dawson and Arrigo came into our room looking for witnesses to write up what happened. Arrigo pointed to five dudes, including Jersey, and told them to come out to the officers' desk.

"This is the GED class. The five of you should be able to write a statement in perfect English," said Arrigo, before he walked back out with his partner.

Everyone in the house knew what the COs wanted. Those dudes were supposed to write how Jessup picked up his hands to Arrigo. That Arrigo popped him in self-defense. And if they really wanted to score points with the COs, they'd put in the made-up part about Jessup catching Arrigo in the eye.

Four of those dudes jumped up and were happy to write. Demarco stared every one of them down, without saying a word as they walked to the door.

But Jersey still had his ass in a chair.

"I don't work for po-lice," Jersey said. "No way. No how."

"You're all rats," somebody called to those dudes on their way out.

"And we're gonna get our cheese right now," one of them answered.

Most dudes would have been down with Five-O, too.

Jessup was fucked anyway you looked at it. The COs would write it up the way they wanted, and that's all that really mattered.

Dudes were just buying the COs' insurance and trying to get something extra for themselves. Maybe it would be phone time or seconds on food at the mess hall. But a taste for little things like that keeps inmates from standing together, and lets the COs get away with a lot of shit.

Dawson came back to the door and barked, "Jersey, are you writing or not?"

Jersey just shook his head and Dawson went on to the next room.

That was the biggest thing I'd seen Jersey do. I was proud of him for not digging Jessup a deeper hole.

Demarco even shook Jersey's hand in front of the class and told him, "I respect that!"

Dawson walked back with Brick stuck to his heels.

"Sanchez," barked Brick, moving his finger like a pencil. "Come outside and help me write a statement."

Sanchez left with his head down. But I didn't hold it against him. I understood the kind of stranglehold Brick had on him.

After a while, Carter called us out of school and we deuced it up in the hall. Dawson and Arrigo were sitting at the officers' desk going over the statements, making sure they all fit together.

When we got back to the house the COs took the count. Even with Jessup getting fixed up at the clinic, I was still Forty. His number just got passed over like he didn't exist. The count jumped from twenty-eight to thirty, and everything else stayed the same.

Another CO came to take Arrigo's post because he was injured.

Then Arrigo went to a hospital out in the world for his eye. But he should have gone to Bellevue to have his brain checked out instead. I wondered if Arrigo would tell his family what *really* happened, or if he would act like some hero who saved the principal from a hard and crazy inmate.

CHAPTER
33

We found out where Mrs. Daniels went in a hurry. Just after Johnson came on duty, two officers from Internal Affairs showed up at the house. They were checking on a report of inmate abuse, wanting to interview a bunch of kids.

"I don't like it, but I can't stop you," Johnson told the officers, cold as ice.

That gave dudes an idea of how Johnson was going to look at anyone who opened his mouth too much.

First, those two IA officers talked to us all together in the dayroom on the north side. They told us that everything we said would be on the down-low, and our names wouldn't show up anywhere. They explained what "reasonable force" meant, and we all laughed out loud.

"Do the officers in this house ever hit inmates when they're angry?" asked one of them.

Johnson was just around the corner with his ears tuned in, and he had plenty of snitches on his payroll to hear anything he couldn't.

So kids kept clammed up tight, and all you could hear was the sound of the ceiling fans turning. What did those two expect? If you dished any dirt on the COs, IA would have to change your house. That was like getting kicked in the ass for doing Corrections a favor. Nobody was that fucking dumb.

Then those two officers talked to every inmate in the house, one by one. But everybody on the north side was watching from their beds, and most dudes being interviewed didn't even want you to see their mouths moving.

When it was my turn, one of the officers looked me over and said, "That cut's still pretty new. You must know something about violence in the Sprungs."

I couldn't tell if that was a question. And they both looked at me like it was my turn to say something.

Finally, I said, "I didn't get cut in the Sprungs."

"Well, we can't hear anything about that then," said the other one.

I sat there burning. I was thinking, *fuck these dudes*. All they care about is their damn report. At least Arrigo didn't front. He was a hard-on CO and he made sure that you knew it, too. These two were just another bullshit part of the system that pretended to be something else. Since it didn't fit their report, maybe this cut on my face wasn't even real.

"Did any COs force or coerce inmates to write statements about what happened today?" one of them asked. "You know that *coerce* could mean to bribe with an extra privilege?"

I sat there looking at him like he was a damn dictionary. But I wouldn't even give an answer. I didn't want to fall into any more traps or holes.

After the officers left, Johnson had a big smile on his face. I even heard him singing a little, and he put the phones out almost an hour early that night as a reward for us.

At supper, Sanchez walked along next to Brick. They talked on the low all the way back to the house. I thought Brick might be laying out a new plan to run the phones, but Sanchez was having a lot to say. And I knew his interest in Brick's business stopped at what he owed.

I was surprised when Sanchez and Brick met with the Spanish dude from the midnight suicide watch. They all went into the bathroom together three different times that night, while Barnett eyed the door. It had to be important because Shaky was nowhere near the action. He was tied to Brick's bed counting merchandise in the store, over and over again.

Then Jessup came back from the clinic with a couple of escorts. Corrections was packing him up to a new house. They couldn't leave him here, where the COs were being investigated for beating his ass.

He looked like there was a ripe plum stuffed under his right eye. Dudes wanted to know if he filed charges against Arrigo.

"You makin' it hot for them, Toothpick?" asked one of the house snitches.

If he wasn't, that meant Mrs. Daniels was making moves against the COs by herself.

The escorts flipped out and wouldn't let anyone within ten feet of him after that. They called for Johnson, and he sent everyone into the dayroom.

On the way out, Jessup looked back at us and shook his head, "No."

Now the COs could figure out how much Mrs. Daniels had taught *them*.

The snitches reported back to Johnson and he cursed her and the rest of the teachers up and down.

"I couldn't stand teachers when I was in school, and it's still that way," Johnson growled. "Don't even mention that school in front of me from now on."

It was almost lights-out when Sanchez finally got back to his bed. He sank into the mattress without taking off his clothes or even his shoes. I might have thought that he was planning to make a break for it. Only I could see that the things on his mind had him weighed down like a cement block. He looked too tired and worn-out to even think about running.

Sanchez didn't say anything to me. He just stared up at the ceiling until the lights went out.

WEDNESDAY, JUNE 17

CHAPTER
34

We walked into the school trailer, and right away, kids went to see if Mrs. Daniels was in her room. But there wasn't any sign of her. The blackboard in her room was blank and the top of her desk was empty.

There was a big, orange sheet of paper hanging on the wall in the hallway. Kids wondered what *that* was about, and it was news to the COs, too.

Officer Carter looked it over, and then he read it out loud.

"Attention all Sprung students—attend the circus at Madison Square Garden next week. See Mr. Costa to sign up!"

"An excellent opportunity," Carter added in a serious voice. "That's something I would take advantage of if I were in your shoes. But I'm not. I have to work for a living."

Ms. Armstrong had a grin on her face and said, "It's always something with these teachers."

Dawson took the kids from Mrs. Daniels's room and split them up into different classes. Then he hollered, "Don't forget to bring me back some cotton candy. Now get to class!"

Demarco was handing out magazines like *Time* and *Newsweek* as we came into the room.

"What happened to Mrs. Daniels?" a kid asked.

"I'll get to that," answered Demarco.

"Say word, you can take us to the circus?" somebody else asked.

"I'll get to that later, too," Demarco said. "First, find the table of contents and read the articles I circled. Just because report cards came out yesterday, don't think that we're through learning here. There are two days of school left and you're all going to be reading."

No one could settle down. Kids were either buzzing about Mrs. Daniels or the trip to the circus. Most dudes thought the circus bit was a gag, but they still wanted to hear it from Demarco.

"I'll go," said Ritz. "I don't care if I have to be shackled in front of people. I'll be out in the world for a day. That's all that counts."

"You are one dumb white boy to believe that shit!" Jersey snapped.

"All right," Demarco said. "I can see we're not going to get anything done until I talk about this."

Just as Demarco got into it, Carter came to the door with Shaky. And Carter had his hand on Shaky's shoulder to keep him from bouncing up and down with excitement.

"I'm sorry to disturb your class, Mr. Costa," said Carter. "This one can't live without signing up for the circus trip right now. I want to make sure he gets a front-row seat with the rest of the clowns."

I just kept looking at Demarco's face. He was playing it as straight as he could. And I almost started to believe that we were going to the circus.

"I arranged it with the Department of Education and the Department of Corrections for next week," Demarco said. "There's room for twenty students and two COs. No one gets shackled, but you all have to promise not to escape. Remember, if somebody takes off we'll never get a trip like this again."

The way he told that story hooked a couple more kids. If he was fishing for herbs, he had plenty of bites. Anyone who had it figured out was already having a good laugh. The others would probably be laughing at themselves later. And I guess that was the whole point. Demarco was trying to keep us loose after Jessup took that beating yesterday.

Then Demarco turned to the other subject.

"As some of you have figured out already, Mrs. Daniels is out there doing what she feels she *has* to do. Everybody makes their own choices in life. This is hers, and that's all I'm going to say."

"This is where I'll step out, Mr. Costa," said Carter, annoyed. "I know you have to cover for your colleague to some extent, but that woman doesn't understand what it means to watch somebody's back."

When class was over, Demarco had seven names for his

trip to the circus. Shaky's name was right at the top, and that should have showed those other six dudes something right there. Two of the kids who put their names down didn't believe Demarco at all.

"I got nothing to lose," one of them said. "And what if it's true?"

Carter probably left thinking that he helped play us for real assholes. But that was *his* game. I could feel how much Demarco cared about us through his whole circus routine. And he didn't make fun of the kids he'd snagged with it either. He even let Shaky stay till the end of class, teaching him how to use a table of contents.

"All I can tell you is that we're going to have a lot of fun at the circus," said Demarco as he left. "And everybody who didn't sign up can have fun on Rikers Island that day instead."

Sanchez sat silent and didn't crack a smile through the whole show. Then after Demarco and Shaky left, he told the class in an even voice, "The teachers won't even be here next week. They're all on summer vacation."

That put an end to Demarco's gag right there. But everybody made a promise not to tell Shaky or the kids in the other rooms. We were the GED class and were supposed to be smarter than other dudes.

Sanchez had already gotten word from Dawson. He was shipping north tomorrow morning and was supposed to pack all his shit tonight. He'd lasted almost three weeks on Rikers after copping a plea. Most dudes are gone in about a week. But

Sanchez still couldn't find anything to be happy about. And when he told me, his face was flat against the desk like it was his last day on earth.

Halfway through Miss Archer's class, Sanchez said to me, "I'll bet they don't have anything like her upstate. An angel like that couldn't last with those hard-up bastards. Some of those dudes haven't touched a woman in ten years. Sooner or later, they'd jump her ass like a kangaroo."

We both laughed, even though it wasn't funny.

Then he whispered to me low, with his hand cupped over my ear, "I cut a deal with Brick and the Spanish dude from the midnight suicide watch."

Sanchez was going to fake a hanging in the bathroom that night, way after lights-out. The dude from the watch was going to have a bedsheet waiting for him in one of the stalls. Sanchez would wrap it around the hot water pipe and stand on a sink. Brick was going to eyeball the bathroom door, making sure the midnight dude was the first one to find him hanging there.

The dude would call for help, and the COs would come running and cut Sanchez down with that hooked blade they carry on their belts. That way no one could say it wasn't for real. The dude from the watch would get a $150 reward put into his account for saving somebody's ass. He'd split the money with Brick to cover what Sanchez still owed from juggling. Then Sanchez could do his time at Bellevue Hospital under observation in the mental ward, instead of going into that jungle upstate.

I didn't like any part of it. I told him that he should quit on the whole idea. But Sanchez had his mind made up that it was the only way out for him.

I didn't believe it could be any better for Sanchez in Bellevue. Most of those dudes had to be really sick in the head and out of control.

"The COs are on point all the time in a place like that," he explained. "They have to be to make sure nothing happens. Besides, they'll all be fucking crazy in there, and I'm not. It'll be easy to play their game."

I asked Sanchez about Mr. Green, the guidance counselor.

"That's going to be the worst part," he said. "I know he's going to take it personal. I like him a lot, and I'm gonna hate for him to feel like he couldn't do his job right."

It was hard to look at Sanchez the rest of the day and keep quiet.

Every time I saw Demarco pass in the hall, I wanted to tell him about Sanchez. I wouldn't tell a CO, but I could tell Demarco. I just didn't think Sanchez was going to do himself any good with this shit. But like Demarco said about Mrs. Daniels, everybody makes their own choices in life.

I thought about giving Sanchez up all the way until we walked out of the school trailer. Then it was over with. I played the jail game, deciding to keep my mouth shut. It was just another choice.

CHAPTER
35

fficer Carter took the count back at the house. Sanchez was thirty-nine, and I was forty. It had been that way since I got to the Sprungs. Only nothing stays the same for too long on Rikers Island. I was waiting for Friday and the possibility of home, like a kid waits on a Christmas present he's almost positive he's getting. But if I could have asked for presents ahead of time, Sanchez not having any real drama that night would have been at the top of my list.

Sanchez wouldn't show me the setup in the bathroom. He was afraid Brick would find out I knew his business and cancel the whole thing. So I went in there on my own to scope it out.

I found the sink that was under the hot water pipe.

Some kid was scrubbing his socks and drawers there, and it was filled with black water. The pipe was all rusty, and I didn't even think it could hold Sanchez. His weight might rip that pipe right out of the wall or break it clean in two. Then he'd flood the house in the middle of the night.

The COs would kick his ass good as a going-away present over something big like that.

I looked into one of the metal mirrors, thinking about how shook Sanchez must be to get himself into this shit. Like life in Bellevue was going to be some sort of dream. He should just sit his ass down on that bus and go upstate. How much worse than Rikers could it be?

Then I studied my own face, and was ready to smack myself in the mouth for even thinking I had something to say.

What did I know about anything?

Dudes could pick up on how this place kicked my ass from a mile away.

So what if people thought Sanchez tried to kill himself or that he was too scared to go upstate? All that could change or wear off when he got older.

My mark was going to stay with me like a neon sign, blinking, RIKERS HERB! RIKERS PUNK! RIKERS THUG!

Sanchez and Brick stuck close together for the rest of the afternoon, watching TV in the dayroom. They didn't talk much at all. Brick was going over his accounts, and Sanchez was staring at the screen. It didn't matter if the program or a commercial was on. Sanchez's expression never changed. It was just cold and blank.

At supper, Sanchez was sitting at a table in the front of the mess hall with Brick, and I couldn't get close. But I saved my milk and orange for him. When we got back to the house

I snuck them into his bucket. He might not eat for a while before they took him to Bellevue from the clinic. So I thought he should stuff himself tonight. I was probably the first reverse sneak thief that Rikers Island had ever seen.

Sanchez got back to his bed and laid down.

He saw what was at the top of his bucket and looked over at me.

"What'd I do to deserve this?" he asked, as he grabbed for the orange and started peeling away the skin.

"For all the help and info you gave me here," I answered.

After the outside peel was gone, he picked away at the stringy white threads on the outside. It took him almost five minutes to get that orange just right. But when Sanchez was finished, it was nothing but the fruit.

"Here's for all the times you listened to me," he said, ripping the orange in half.

We both took our time enjoying it.

Then I emptied my bucket and put it halfway between our beds.

We made a contest of trying to spit the seeds into it.

Jersey saw us and got all pissed off.

"You know the house gang's gonna get blamed for your bad aim and have to clean up this mess," Jersey said.

Sanchez broke into a half-smile and told him, "That's what the *housemaids* get paid for, son."

I felt better to think he wasn't so tight, and could laugh a little.

When it got late, Sanchez started to walk laps around the

house. He would circle around the dayroom, past the beds and phones, and up to the officers' station. Then he'd start all over again.

He never once walked into the bathroom or even looked inside.

It was almost lights-out, and he hadn't even packed up.

"What about all your stuff?" I asked, once he stood still.

He just looked at it and said, "Later, for that shit."

It was the first time I ever saw Sanchez with a watch. He must have got it from Brick. That way they could all be organized. It wouldn't be much of a plan if everybody was just guessing when to move.

The COs got the house to bed and turned out the lights. It felt like my insides were starting to freeze up solid in the dark. And the waiting that night felt as long as my five months on the Island put together.

THURSDAY, JUNE 18

CHAPTER

36

After what felt like a couple of hours, I heard Officer Johnson cursing up front. His tour was over and he should have been gone by now. He'd probably got stuck doing overtime when another CO called in sick or something. And having Johnson around wasn't good news if you were trying to run some kind of game in the house.

I was lying flat on my stomach looking over at Sanchez. He had his back up against the pillow and his eyes wide open. Sanchez wasn't even blinking much. But every time I closed my eyes, I saw him with a sheet around his neck hanging from that pipe, trying to call out for help. So I kept my eyes open, too, and wondered about the time.

Soon Brick started making little throat-clearing noises, like he was ready to go. Sanchez never budged or even bothered looking at his watch. Then the dude from the midnight crew walked through and kicked the leg on Sanchez's bed.

None of it moved him.

Sanchez sat there for a long time. Then he jumped out of bed all at once. He headed straight for the bathroom and disappeared inside. I figured it would take a while for him to set everything up. So I started counting Mississippis in my head. I was up to three hundred when the dude from the midnight crew walked into the bathroom. But he came right back out again, and I couldn't figure out what was going on.

I was worried about Sanchez and wanted to go rushing in there. I didn't give a shit about their plan. I just wanted to make sure that he was okay.

As many times as I ran it over in my head, I never got up because another side of me kept saying, *He's doing what he has to do.*

At five hundred Mississippi, the dude went back inside.

The sound of my heart beating got louder with every number I counted off.

Then, suddenly, that midnight suicide dude busted out screaming for the COs.

"Help! COs! Help!" he yelled, with his voice running through me cold, like a ghost.

It wasn't the scream of a kid that was running some scam.

It sounded too real, and out of control.

I ran to the bathroom and got there with the COs and a bunch of other kids on my heels. I looked up and Sanchez was hanging from the pipe with the sheet wrapped tight around his neck. His face was horrible and twisted. He looked nothing like the kid I knew, and I would have sworn it was somebody else.

I never saw a body in so much pain. And I almost heaved right there.

Officer Johnson bulled his way through the bodies at the door.

When he saw Sanchez hanging there he started hollering, "You idiot kid! Look what you fucking did! Look at what you fucking went and did!"

The other COs pushed kids back outside and the alarm went off.

But I just spun back around and stayed in the bathroom, close to the wall.

I watched Johnson cut Sanchez down from the pipe and loosen the sheet around his neck. He put his fingers on Sanchez's throat to feel for a pulse. Then he exploded, pounding his fist on the floor.

"Damn you!" Johnson yelled. "Damn you!"

Johnson hit the floor so hard he split one of the tiles in two.

He saw me standing behind him and smacked me hard in the head.

"You seen enough?" he hollered, with his voice echoing off the walls.

Johnson wrapped one hand around my neck and dragged me out of the bathroom. He passed me off to another CO, and I got pushed into the dayroom with everyone else.

My ears were ringing and I couldn't stand.

I just collapsed to the floor.

Sanchez was gone.

He wasn't going upstate. He wasn't going to the mental ward at Bellevue. And he was never going home again. It didn't make any sense.

Every CO in the Sprungs who wasn't tied to a post rushed to our house. They had kids pinned down at tables in the dayroom. Then the Turtles showed up and rushed a doctor from the clinic straight into the bathroom.

No matter how many COs watched us, they couldn't stop kids from talking. Enough dudes had seen Sanchez hanging there that word spread quick.

For all the bullshit we threw at each other on the Island, no one wanted to see another kid get hurt like that. And no one wanted to believe somebody could really die in the Sprungs. But when they wheeled Sanchez out with a clean white sheet over his head, they could have thrown a sheet over every bullshit threat that kids ever laid down out here, too.

Right then, it seemed like no one wanted anything but peace. And all of a sudden, that dayroom became more like a church than a jail.

Jersey and Ritz came over to where I was sitting on the floor.

"Did you—see him in there?" stuttered Ritz.

I couldn't answer.

They must have been able to tell I had from the look on my face, and didn't ask again. They both sat there next to me, taking turns keeping a hand on my shoulder. And I appreciated that.

Lots of kids had tears in their eyes. But I knew they were crying for more than Sanchez. They were crying for everything we ever did to each other on the streets and in the Sprungs. And they were crying because they were scared of what could happen to them on Rikers Island, too.

I thought about that kid who'd cut me and how I wanted to slice him back. Then I thought about how Mom must have felt when she heard I got cut, and how *his* mother would feel if it happened to *him*.

I just couldn't get the sight of Sanchez hanging there out of my head. How his face was in so much pain.

I knew that Sanchez's mother was already dead. That would be one less mother getting a bad phone call and crying.

Brick was sitting at a table trying to blend into the scenery. He looked more worried than upset. Kids were talking about what happened to Sanchez, and Brick was listening like it was all news to him. I always thought of Brick as just another jail thug running his bullshit games. But right then, I started to hate him with some real heart. Not because his whole fucked-up plan went wrong, but because he didn't give two shits about Sanchez. Even when it all broke down to nothing, he only cared about himself.

I wasn't really sure if Sanchez had killed himself by mistake or not. Maybe something went wrong with the plan, or Sanchez just had enough of everything in his life. I knew that he was scared, and sometimes fear can push you too far.

Unless the dude from the suicide watch came clean, everybody was going to think Sanchez went in there to kill himself, straight-up. The COs had that dude at the officers' desk filling out reports. But I couldn't see him sticking his own neck out for Sanchez now.

I'd already made my choice not to tell Demarco. There was no going back on that. I knew that Sanchez got caught up in the traps and holes on Rikers Island, big-time.

Maybe I did too by keeping my mouth shut.

A couple of kids fell asleep in the dayroom. But most dudes just quit on sleeping that night. The COs didn't let us go back to our beds until every last investigator and photographer had packed up.

Most of the extra COs who got sent to our house that night were respectful. They saw right away that no one was going to wild out. Kids were too shook for that. So they talked to us.

"It's a shame what can happen," said a CO I'd never laid eyes on before. "I got a son almost his age. This cuts deep."

I didn't want to go back to my bed. I didn't want to look over at Sanchez's blanket and pillow anymore. I could see them from the dayroom, and that was close enough for now.

Johnson was still doing paperwork on Sanchez when the morning tour of COs came on. All of them knew what had happened before they even got to the house. They either heard about it at the front gate or at roll call.

I watched Ms. Armstrong walk across the yard through

the windows of the emergency doors. She held her palm flat against her mouth the whole way.

Dawson and Carter came in together. They were both acting stiff and did everything in slow motion that morning.

After an hour or so, Dawson called me up front.

"Forty, you slept next to Sanchez," he said, handing me a plastic laundry bag. "You know what belonged to him. Pack it all up so they can send it to his family. I heard he had an aunt and uncle in the Bronx."

I was about to tell Dawson that I didn't want any part of it, when Brick came up from behind me.

"I can handle it," Brick said, reaching out his hand.

I spun around hard, tightening my grip on the bag. Then I walked right through Brick's shoulder to the beds. I wasn't about to let *him* go through any of it.

Sanchez's bed and bucket were just like he'd left them.

No one was going to sneak-thief from a kid who'd just died.

But I couldn't stand his bed being all messed up. It was like he was coming back from the bathroom to fix it. I even touched his sheet, thinking it might still be warm.

Only it was cold.

I took a deep breath and started to make his bed before I did any of the packing. I took my time with it until all the corners came out even.

I folded Sanchez's clothes and put them into the bag. I didn't know what to do with the leftover food in his bucket, so I started in on his books.

Brick came over and stuck his hand in the bucket. He grabbed the milk I gave Sanchez the night before.

"You can't pack this. It'll go bad," he said, opening it.

I just flipped. I hit that bastard dead square in the chest, and he went straight down.

The COs came charging over and I backed away.

They didn't lay a hand on me. But Dawson grabbed Brick around the collar and threw him on the wall.

"I told *Forty* to pack that boy's shit," said Dawson. "What were you doin' over there? Huh? You got an answer for that? You were doin' business, right? You little grave robber!"

Jersey and Ritz were both giving me the thumbs-up for belting Brick, but I didn't want to get caught up in that. I just went back to packing Sanchez's things.

Ms. Armstrong pulled a chair over to where Brick was holding up the wall. She gave him a speech that lasted the whole time he was there.

"Maybe you heard the words *do unto others*, but they just passed right through your ears," she started out.

Kids were tuned into that and started running Brick down, too.

I didn't think we were going to make it to school that morning. We were already a couple of hours late and it was the last day of classes.

Dawson said we were going over anyway.

"The teachers and the guidance counselor want to talk about last night," he said.

Carter called us to our beds to take the count.

The numbers began to build up slow and I could feel it coming. By the time we hit the thirties, I was holding onto myself tight from the inside.

The kid two beds down said, "thirty-eight."

Then I called out "forty," without any break in between.

CHAPTER 37

Demarco met us at the door to our class. His eyes were swollen, and I could tell he'd been crying. The chairs were in a circle in the middle of the room. I was glad because I didn't have to think about sitting next to Sanchez's empty seat.

The guidance counselor, Mr. Green, was going into rooms and talking to the different classes. But for now, it was just us and Demarco.

"Does anybody want to talk about what they're feeling?" Demarco asked.

Most kids just said it was a shame what happened. They talked about how Sanchez never bothered anybody, and how kids thought he was okay.

I didn't want to say anything out loud. I was afraid that I would have screamed out about how much I really knew.

Lots of kids were getting up to use the bathroom. I got in line, too. No one had wanted to use the one back at the house because of Sanchez. But that had to wear off sooner or later. This was the last day of school, and kids on the north side couldn't hold out from moving their bowels through the summer.

The bathroom in the school trailer is about the size of a closet and has only one toilet. You're in there by yourself, but after two minutes the CO will bang on the door to keep the line moving. I took as much time as I could get, and kept pushing until I felt empty. I was hoping that I could last until the pens tomorrow morning. I didn't think I could ever step inside the bathroom in the house again without seeing Sanchez hanging there.

When I got back to the classroom, Demarco had Sanchez's folder out on his desk.

"Are you all right, Martin?" he asked.

I nodded my head, and deep inside it felt good to hear someone call me by my name.

Then Demarco and me looked through the folder together.

Sanchez's copy of his GED diploma was right on top.

You need a score of 225 to pass. He'd got a 285, making it by plenty. But I guess you could be pretty smart and still get caught up in dumb shit, too.

Carter came in with the guidance counselor, and I was surprised when Carter wanted to talk first. He stepped to the middle of the room and cleared his throat.

"Let me say this," Carter began with his voice cracking. "I know a lot of you think that COs are a bunch of monsters. Right or wrong, sometimes we think the same about you. But what happened to Sanchez last night is bigger than all of that crap. We're here to protect you. I got two kids myself. And I wouldn't want to get a call that something like that happened to one of them. The counselor and teachers are here so you can talk. But remember, this badge doesn't make us monsters. I want you to know that you can talk to the officers in this house, too."

That was the first time I ever saw Carter be real, and not a freaked-out robot. Carter introduced Mr. Green, and he then took a seat with the rest of us.

Green told us about his bid upstate and how he'd seen lots of fucked-up things like what happened to Sanchez.

"You've got to focus yourself on what's ahead. You can either be sad or angry over something like this. You can feel anything you want to feel about it. But you have to stay focused on what's ahead of you. You have to keep it right for you, and your family," Green said.

I could see why Sanchez liked him so much and didn't want to let him down. Green wasn't about any kind of bullshit. He looked kids straight in the eye. And I swear he never once gave the scar on my face a second look.

After he was done talking, I shook his hand for Sanchez.

Demarco told Green, "This is Martin Stokes, a really good student."

Then Green asked about my case, and what I expected to happen. I told Demarco and Green that I was probably going home from court tomorrow. I wanted them to know that I was going to finish school and make something of myself. I didn't care how many other dudes were listening anymore. Nobody in that house was getting in the way of my going home. Nobody!

The COs called us out into the hall. School was over with. We were going to the mess hall, then back to the house. But Demarco asked me to wait a minute. He went back into Sanchez's folder and gave me the copy of his GED diploma.

I hugged Demarco and said, "Thank you."

Dawson was in the hall lining kids up and calling for Brick. He had a visit and there was an escort waiting for him at the officers' desk with Ms. Armstrong.

"I'm gonna refuse that visit," Brick told Dawson.

"Go up to the desk and let them know," Dawson shot back, as he counted kids.

Brick told the escort he wasn't going to the visit floor to see anybody.

"That's the first one of those in a long time," the escort laughed.

"Kids are just ungrateful sometimes," Ms. Armstrong said.

Brick turned back to them and said, "That's my grandmother waiting on me. Last week, she forgot my money. I know her government check doesn't come again until next week. I'm not in the mood just to make small talk with her."

Ms. Armstrong shot out of her chair like she was the judge and jury all rolled up into one. She smacked Brick across the face with an open black hand. He went to the floor on one knee. Then she slapped him in the back of the head even harder.

"You're *going* to see your grandmother," she warned, standing over him. "Aren't you, little boy? You going to see your grandmother because she loves you, and she came all the way to Rikers Island."

The tears were pouring out of Brick's eyes.

"Now get up and go with this officer," Ms. Armstrong demanded.

Brick picked himself up, crying all the while. Then he followed the escort out of the trailer. Kids gave Ms. Armstrong a real cheer. But she didn't want to hear any more about it.

CHAPTER
38

Captain Montenez showed up at the house in street clothes, with his gold badge around his neck. It was his day off, but he came back to the jail when he heard that a kid from the Sprungs had hung up.

"Bad shit only happens when I'm not around to supervise," he told Dawson with a straight face.

Montenez sat down and read every report there was. Then he went off to inspect the bathroom with Dawson. When they got back, Montenez called the carpenters out from the main building. They came on the double with their toolboxes and a shopping cart full of wood.

The COs closed the bathroom because of all the tools that were laid out. They don't want some kid walking off with a screwdriver or a hammer, and then have to search the whole damn house.

Dudes that peeped inside said they were building a cover around the hot water pipe. That way no one could ever slip a bedsheet over it again, like Sanchez did.

The captain grilled the dude from the midnight suicide crew for almost an hour. Then he ran the dude back and forth from the bathroom to replay everything that happened. Every time they disappeared inside, my stomach started to knot up all over again.

After the captain was through with him, that dude got the nerve up to ask about his $150 for finding Sanchez.

Montenez grinned and said, "You have to save somebody to get paid. You don't get any prizes around here for breaking bad news!"

The dude didn't say anything more about it. I guess he saw that it was going nowhere and quit on the whole idea.

I was pissed off at the dude for trying to cash in on Sanchez being dead.

I didn't hold much against him before that. He was only playing his end of the game that night, just like I was by keeping my mouth shut. And I knew that Sanchez killing himself probably had more to do with what was going on inside his own head than any bullshit plan. But I thought it was really fucked-up the way that dude asked to get paid anyway.

When Johnson came on, Montenez was still in the house. Johnson told Montenez that it was the worst thing he'd seen in all his time on the Island.

"I don't need another night like that one," moaned Johnson.

"You go home and just keep thinking about it. To waste a life like that!"

"If it wasn't a kid, you could almost stand it," Montenez said, moving for the front door in his jeans and sneakers.

Jersey and Ritz were both looking at me sideways. They had heard me tell Demarco and Green about going home tomorrow. Jersey was all insulted, wanting to know why I'd been so tight-lipped.

"I understand not putting that news out on the loudspeaker. But we're not the rest of these dudes up in here," he said, pointing to himself and Ritz.

I told him he was right, and that I should have said something. They both came around after a while and shook my hand. And it felt good not to hide it anymore.

"We're a righteous crew, my brothers," said Ritz.

Maybe I hadn't realized how much standing up to Brick really meant to them.

After supper, I called my real house. I knew that Mom would be in court the next day, but I wanted to hear the words come out of her mouth. Just like I wanted to hear my lawyer say that we were all straight with the DA. I wanted everything nailed down, with nothing left to chance. I wanted to hear the judge say, "Have a nice day, and get home safe."

"I'll be there," Mom said.

It had all gone bad three times before. There was almost nothing left that could go wrong, and I was hoping this screwed-up system didn't have any more surprises for me. If there were an earthquake tomorrow that split the courthouse in two, I'd just sit there and let everybody else go running. I'd wait for the system to stamp me GOOD TO GO.

Mom didn't think she'd be able to sleep.

"I'll probably lie awake in bed watching the clock move forward," she said. "Then when it makes it far enough, I'll get up and dress for court."

I didn't mention anything about Sanchez because I didn't want that on her mind, too.

At the end, we didn't get tied up in a lot of *I love yous*. It was just "good night" and "keep your fingers crossed."

But I knew she was worried more about me going through the pens and having beefs than about my case. So I told her I'd keep my head up and stay away from trouble.

Maybe I was trying to convince myself, too.

Brick wasn't anywhere near the phones. He was laying low off the licks he took from Ms. Armstrong. For most of the night, he was either sulking in the dayroom or at his bed going through the store. He was like a ghost now. And kids were probably wondering why they'd put up with his bullshit for so long.

Barnett didn't know if he should hassle kids over the phones, so he just backed off. That's the way it is when you're a doldier and the boss cracks. It leaves you standing in the middle of nowhere, with a lot of enemies.

I felt bad for Shaky. He just kept going around the house saying he couldn't believe Brick really cried. I told Jersey that

Shaky could hold down my spot after I left. But he just made a face and didn't say a word.

After lights-out, I spent a long time looking over at San-chez's empty bed. When the new jacks rolled into the house there would be another "thirty-nine" to take his spot.

I was glad I wouldn't be around to see it.

There'd be another kid to take my bed, too. And I already felt sad for him and his family, and for what he might have done to somebody to get locked up on Rikers Island.

FRIDAY, JUNE 19

CHAPTER
39

It was five o'clock in the morning when the CO coming on duty stumbled down the rows of beds, counting. It was Ms. Armstrong. She had a cup of coffee in one hand and was touching each sleeping kid with the other. She mumbled the numbers softly and her voice went up and down like a lullaby.

"Thirty-six . . . thirty-seven . . . thirty-eight," she counted.

She got to Sanchez's empty bed and said, "Bless that child's soul, Lord."

Then she saw my face looking back at hers.

"Forty," she whispered and touched my shoulder.

I had put on my clean pants and shirt before she even started. I was just lying there waiting for her to round up the courts.

"I see you're ready this morning, honey," she said, and kept moving.

When she made her way back past my bed, I got up and followed her to the front of the house. There were a couple of other dudes headed to court, too. But they were either still getting dressed or cleaning up in the bathroom.

Ms. Armstrong pulled my card from the box.

I sat down in an open chair, and she said, "Stand up, please. This is not a hangout."

I jumped up like my own mother had told me to move.

Then she looked at the unscarred face on my card, and her eyes got sad.

"How did this happen, Martin?" she asked.

When she called me "Martin," everything I'd been holding back just wanted to come flooding out.

"I got cut on the way back from court. They wanted some other dude, but I got caught in the middle," I answered.

She shook her head, and I really believed she was sorry.

That was the first time I had told anyone on the Island. I never thought I would breathe a word of it inside the house. Only the inmates on that bus, the COs who saw it go down, and the kid who cut me knew the story. But I wasn't going to play Ms. Armstrong out in the cold, not now.

She flipped that card out on the desk, and I prayed it would be the last time anyone would think of me as "Forty."

"Once you make it home, I don't ever want to see you out here again," she said.

She was always talking to kids about her son in junior high. I thought he was lucky to have a mother who was a CO.

He could hear all about what it was really like in jail. Then it would be his own damn fault if he didn't listen.

When the other dudes got up front, Ms. Armstrong dropped that kind of sensitive talk with me. I knew she was being respectful of my privacy.

One dude was so nervous about his case he couldn't stop talking. He replayed the whole thing a couple of times.

I couldn't concentrate on anything except what was ahead of me, and his words just flew right past. I was busy looking out at the house, thinking about all that had happened here. I was thinking how I never wanted to see this place again. But I knew that I was going to carry it with me forever, like this mark on my face.

The only thing that stuck with me about that dude's case was Ms. Armstrong telling him, "Pray for the best, child. Just pray for the best."

My kidneys were starting to burn, but I wasn't going into that bathroom. I just wanted to hold out until I got to the pens.

The escort picked us up. We walked through the front doors of the house and it was over. Sprung #3 was behind me now. Then we moved across the yard, past the school trailer. I thought about Demarco trying to prove he knew every kid's first name. That lifted me up inside. Maybe he wasn't the best teacher I ever had for teaching verbs and nouns. But he was the best kind a kid on Rikers Island could run into. He was nothing but real, and he understood how kids were feeling.

We stopped for inmates at some of the mods inside the main building, and our group doubled in size. I began to feel tight about all those other dudes. But I told myself, *It's just the same old building game. Dudes want to look hard and walk tough. That's all it is.*

In the transportation yard, the COs patted everyone down.

I was shackled by the wrist and foot to one of the adults. He looked calm enough, and I was relieved to see that he was my partner. But when the shackles closed shut, that whole slashing came roaring back at me. I almost couldn't breathe and my heart was pumping out of control.

My legs and feet turned numb and I could hardly walk. That adult tried to pull me along a little, but I couldn't go any faster. The sweat was falling off my face and I probably looked like some dude facing the electric chair, instead of going home.

"Ease up, kid. You're making this hard," my partner said.

I wanted to scream out at the top of my lungs for the COs to take those damn shackles off. But they wouldn't have listened. They're deaf to shit like that. And I was so shook that maybe nothing would have come out of my mouth, even if I'd opened it.

We got on the bus and I was sitting next to a window. I closed my eyes tight and listened to the sound of the big engine cranking up. Then the bus started to roll past the checkpoints to the main gate. I counted them off blind in my head with every stop.

The Rikers Island Bridge came up fast, and I could feel the slight incline as we picked up speed. I finally opened my eyes, and there was nothing out the window but blue water and sky.

The bus hit the streets of East Elmhurst and rolled toward the highway.

I kept opening and closing my hands, trying to get the feeling back into my fingers. I'd made the trip from Rikers to the courthouse and back three times before. Every bump and turn was part of my memory. But I couldn't find my way now. Everything was out of place. The sweat was stinging my eyes and I kept seeing buildings I would have sworn we'd already passed.

The dude sitting behind me moved to get himself straight, and I nearly jumped out of my seat.

It felt like it was a hundred and fifty degrees and that bus had become an oven.

We turned from Queens Boulevard into the courthouse yard.

The COs ran us off the bus and through the system quick.

But that fever burning inside of me didn't stop until one of them turned a key and those shackles finally came off.

Once I got put into the pen, I headed for the toilet in the corner. I must have stood there for almost two minutes emptying my bladder.

After that, I found a quiet spot in the back, near the wall.

The pen filled up fast, and was crowded as anything.

By nine o'clock, the COs started to call a few inmates out for their cases. I was just waiting out my time, hoping I was getting ready to walk free.

Then one of the COs came up to the pen with some kid in a headlock. Another officer turned the key and pushed open the gate. Together they shoved his ass inside.

"Start any more trouble," the CO told him, "and I'll chain you to a parking meter outside like a dog."

The kid said some smart-mouthed shit back. But I wasn't listening to his words. I was glued to his face. It was the kid who'd cut me. I kept looking to make sure. I needed to be positive. Then I saw the spiderweb tattoo on his neck.

Anything hard that was ever inside of me came boiling up to the top. My fists squeezed tight, and my brain was all static.

Some guys I'd never seen before were zeroed in on that kid, too.

Then one of them said something to him.

I was working my way closer to them, when it all broke loose.

Three of those guys grabbed the kid and rushed him to the back while the others blocked the COs' view up front.

It was like the devil had sent him to me, special delivery.

There were hands around his throat, and his head was pushed hard against the wall.

"You're the one who cut my cousin Frankie," growled one of those guys. "You think I wouldn't recognize you?"

The kid was struggling to breathe and get loose, and I could hear him squeal. I was sizing up the bunch of them. Numbers didn't mean shit to me anymore.

I stepped over to where they had him pinned.

"Maybe you don't remember this face," I said.

My voice took two of those dudes by surprise and they jumped back. That let the tattooed kid tangle himself up good with the guy who was fighting for his cousin.

They both had a solid grip on each other now, and neither could break free from the other.

"This prick cut you, too?" asked the guy that was tied to him.

But I couldn't answer. I was hooked on looking through that tattooed kid.

I could see everything working inside of him. His blood was pumping hard and the veins up and down his spider-webbed neck were ready to explode.

"Give it to 'im," the guy grunted, pushing his chin at me.

One of his friends cupped his right hand and brought it over to mine. He pushed a razor blade flat into my palm. I closed a fist around it tight and felt how cold it was.

I moved the blade between my thumb and fingers. Every bit of the last five months on Rikers was crammed into that space with it.

I raised that hand as high as my cheek, with that spider-web in front of me.

A piece of light hit off the blade, shining into my eyes.

I could feel the kid's heart go numb and see it in his face as I followed through.

Every trap and hole this fucked-up system had to offer was right there.

I was standing on a ledge they'd set up for me out in the middle of nowhere. And the only thing I had to fall back on were the people who'd tried like hell to save me.

For a split-second I thought about Mom and I saw her face.

I crashed my elbow into the kid's forehead, knocking him loose from that other guy. The blade went flying across the floor. I smothered that tattooed kid in my arms, wrestling him to the front of the pen.

"COs! COs!" I screamed, and they came busting in.

In a split second, I'd decided that nobody was going to get cut today.

They dragged us out of the pen, pulling us apart.

No matter which way they turned me, I kept fighting to look at that tattooed kid's face. I wanted to see everything he was feeling. I wanted to see what it was like for him to walk that ledge, too.

He owed me plenty, and I didn't want to be cheated out of a thing.

We both got put on the wall.

I couldn't tell the tears from the sweat pouring off his face.

And I felt like I'd collected enough from him to let it go.

CHAPTER
40

The COs sent me back to the pen alone. I don't know where they put the kid with that spiderweb tattoo, or what they did to him. Those guys who knew each other had gone in different directions inside the pen. There was a blade on the floor and none of them wanted to be connected to it.

I stood at the bars like a rock, harder and cleaner than I'd ever been before. My eyes searched for the dude who'd stood up for his cousin. He was in the back sitting on a bench with his head to the floor.

I stayed on him until he finally looked up and saw me standing there.

He looked more scared than angry now.

"You owe me, too," I blurted out.

I had just picked us both up and stepped around one deep hole. The kind that's so dark you might never find your way out.

A CO called my name and opened the door for me.

An officer cuffed my hands, but I wasn't going to sweat that now. Whatever had me so tight about being shackled before was either gone or I had it beat down to nothing.

We crisscrossed the hallways through the courthouse. I was praying we weren't going to one of the conference rooms. I didn't want to hear any more bad news about my case from Miss Thompson. But we rounded the last corner and walked out into the front of a courtroom. I stepped around the flag and saw the rows of benches in the back. Mom was sitting in the first one. And she raised herself up off the bench a little when she saw me walk through that door.

Miss Thompson was waiting at the lawyers' desk. I hadn't seen her since before I'd got cut. She looked as uncomfortable as could be, watching me.

When the officer took off the cuffs, she stood up and shook my hand.

"I'm sorry about what happened to you," she said, looking at my face.

"Just get me home," I said.

I looked over at the DA. He was a skinny black dude in a suit and tie. He probably wouldn't last two minutes on the Island. But that was the dude who had every kid on Rikers shook. That's because he had the power, and held a good part of your life in his hands.

The DA could drop the charges against you or push all the way for the max. He could threaten you with serious time over bullshit, and might get you to cop out to something you didn't even do.

And before you could decide anything, you had to figure out if your legal aid lawyer needed a Seeing Eye dog or not.

The judge came in and everyone stood up.

He was wearing a black robe and looked old and tired climbing up to his high desk. He cleaned his glasses while an officer read out my case number, name, and the charge against me.

"Counselors?" the judge asked.

There was a meeting up at the judge's desk with the DA and Miss Thompson. They talked for a while, and I kept looking over my shoulder to see if Mom was all right.

Miss Thompson came back and said we were all straight.

"When they ask you, just plead guilty," she said.

So I did.

I felt bad about myself when the word "guilty" came out of my mouth.

And I felt even worse for Mom.

The judge said that a year of probation and a drug program on Saturday mornings would make the state square with me. But I didn't know that anything was ever going to make me even with the system again.

"Did you learn anything from this, young man?" asked the judge.

I nodded my head and said, "Yes, sir."

But I knew that he didn't understand anything about what I'd picked up. Maybe he knew all those law books cold, but he probably didn't know shit about how it really worked. He couldn't know, sitting way up there. It was too clean and safe, like out of some storybook. A book where you only lose the time a judge gives you, and nothing else.

He didn't understand what happens to kids on Rikers Island. He didn't see them get cut or beat up. He didn't hear the COs threaten to whip their asses. And he didn't see Sanchez hang himself around the neck with a bedsheet.

The system wouldn't let him see any of that, or they might not be able to keep him walking on their leash.

I wondered if that judge kept count of how many black and Spanish kids he'd sent away. Did he ever study up on why all the white dudes with paid lawyers never spend a day on Rikers Island? Or maybe the system picked him for a judge because he was *color-blind*.

I know a lot of kids do dumb shit and deserve to be locked up.

I just couldn't figure out how so many kids from the same neighborhoods got *screwed up* and turned *bad* all at the same time.

I signed some legal papers.

And by the time I put down the pen, Mom was holding me.

We were hugging each other so tight I don't know how we made it out of the courtroom. But we did. We made it out to the street, down into the subway, and home.

Turn the page for a glimpse of
Paul Volponi's next book:

CROSSING LINES

garbage, and you don't even know it. I understand that now. That it can take a long time to get your stuck-up nose down to where it belongs, down to where you can smell your own stink.

The first time I ever laid eyes on Alan was late last May, in gym class. Junior year.

It was during the warm-up, and we were all running laps around the red rubber track circling the athletic field.

I was pushing myself to keep pace with Rodney Bishop and James Godfrey, two speedy wide receivers on the football team with me. We were coming up quick on Alan from behind, as his blond hair bounced against his boney shoulder blades. He must have heard our footsteps coming, because he cut from the inside lane onto the grass to let us go past.

"Oh, shit! Did you see that fag?" asked Bishop, real loud. "I swear, 1 thought that new kid was gonna be a chick from behind."

"Yeah, you were about to holler at that homo and ask him out," cracked Godfrey.

I looked back over my shoulder and saw that Alan had stopped.

I knew he'd heard Bishop, and I thought that expression on his face—somewhere between being really pissed off and ready to cry—was funny as hell.

"Nah, I knew that was a faggot all along," Bishop defended himself. "How 'bout you, Adonis? Did you know?"

"Are you kidding?" I said as we leaned into the turn, three abreast. "I knew from fifty yards back. That's why he runs so slow. His butt hurts."

"That why *you've* been getting slower?" Godfrey cackled at Bishop. "Your butt hurts, too?"

"That's *you*. I'll show you slow," Bishop said, turning on the jets and pulling away.

Godfrey sprinted after him.

I tried to go with them. But a big offensive lineman like me couldn't keep up, and they just left me in their dust.

Alan had just transferred into Central High, and I'd

have called it a rough beginning. I remember some of the other guys taking jabs at Alan, making comments about his tight-ass pants, asking him if he'd transferred from a high school in San Francisco, or calling him a fag to his face.

I had run my mouth at him a few times, too, even though he never did anything to me or anybody else I knew.

Other than that one time on the running track, I never saw Alan let a nasty remark go.

He'd usually come right back at you with a sharp tongue, waving his finger around and saying things like, "If you want to be judge and jury, you should stand in front of the mirror more. That way you can talk to the source of your problem."

He even called a cafeteria table full of football players I was sitting at "pigs," when one of us whistled at him as a joke.

That kind of insult was almost funny coming from him, like *he* had the right to put himself over anybody.

After that, whenever guys on the team saw Alan, we'd scrunch up our snouts like pigs and snort at him.

Then the teachers and deans couldn't get on us for using "inappropriate" language.

I was convinced that hostility between Alan and the football team was all Alan's fault.

He could be gay if he wanted. There were probably some other kids at our school who were *that way*, too, or leaning there.

But they didn't make a show out of it, like Alan did. So nobody really cared.

He didn't have to flit around the hallways drawing attention to himself, swinging his hips and arms like a raging fem.

And whatever shit Alan took on account of it, I figured he deserved.

Alan didn't have problems with most of the girls at school. I guess that's because he was almost one of them. He'd usually be hanging around with a group of females, even good-looking ones. That got a lot of *real* guys even more annoyed, feeling like they couldn't go over and make a move on one of them with him there. It would be too weird.

When school broke for the summer, at the end of

June, I didn't see Alan again for a couple of months.

I didn't know what dudes like him did with their vacations. Maybe he was sitting in the library all day. Maybe he got a summer job serving cappuccino in a coffeehouse, or was at home plucking his eyebrows. Or maybe he hung around some men's room in a public park waiting to hook up with another queer.

I just knew wherever Alan was, I wasn't.

And that was perfect with me.

1

I didn't see Alan again until early September. It was the Tuesday after Labor Day, on the first day of our senior year.

He was in my English and gym classes, first and last period, every day.

I made sure to sit on the other side of the room from him in English. And in gym, I was safe because I changed my clothes in the section of lockers reserved for varsity athletes, where I'd been changing for two years already, and where Alan was nowhere in sight.

I never figured on Alan jumping up into my life past being in those two classes. But he did.

It was just after one o'clock, but the first day of school was already over. We'd had a half day, with twenty-minute classes to get our program cards signed. I was walking across the athletic field with some of my teammates, heading towards the weight room—a beat-up trailer that used to store textbooks before it got converted into something useful. We were going to pump some serious iron and get ready for our first football game of the season the following week, after putting in a month of practices in the heat of August.

"Spy what's up on the bleachers," Bishop said. "It's Chick City. Just look at all those lovelies. There must be forty of them."

"Is that some kind of meeting they're having?" asked Ethan, our quarterback and team captain. "I don't remember them asking my permission. It's never good when that many girls get together. All they do is compare notes and bitch about us."

Ethan was six-foot-two, the same height as me. Only he already had the kind of body I was lifting weights to get. His shoulders were as wide as mine, but his waist was probably seven inches smaller and his muscles were really cut.

Almost every girl I ever heard pass a comment about

him used the word *hot*, even if they did call him a prick, too.

And that's what I wanted.

"They're probably deciding how far to go on a first date," said Godfrey.

"Send 'em a memo from me—it's either all the way or the highway," said Ethan, pounding a football between his huge paws. "I got a no-tease policy."

"Yeah, put out or get out of the car and walk home," echoed Godfrey. "No middle ground on that."

Right away, my eyes settled on Melody Singer, a senior, who was sitting in the second row. I'd hung out with her a few times over the summer.

The first time was with a bunch of other kids, including my sister, Jeannie, who was a year younger than me. Jeannie understood that I had it bad for Melody, so she set it up for me to tag along to this lightweight kegger. I was the only jock in the crowd, so I knew I'd stood out. Hardly anybody there, except for me, had more than two small cups of beer. And no one puked or got loud.

I spent the whole night zeroed in on Melody, paying

attention to what she said about a bunch of books I'd never read and the kind of movies I hadn't seen.

I'd wanted to get next to Melody for a long time. It was more than her just being pretty. She was smart, too. And there was something about Melody I couldn't explain, something that jumped up and hit me over the head every time I laid eyes on her. But she usually had more guys falling over her than I could count. So the competition was always stiff, and I'd never made a real move on her before.

Besides, I'd heard her say around school, "Football players and wrestlers are basically pinheads. I don't like guys whose attitudes are bigger than their brains."

But I knew that Jeannie had put in a good word for me, and I made sure to agree with everything Melody said that night about those books and movies, even though I had to fake it.

It all paid off for me a few days later, when Melody pulled into the service station where I had a summer job. She'd just got her license and her parents had bought her a used Chevy Cavalier.

"It has a few little hiccups," Melody told me, wrapping some strands of her long brown hair around a finger. "The previous owner said something about plugs and belts needing to be changed soon. Only I'm not exactly sure which ones. I'm totally clueless about anything that takes a screwdriver or a wrench."

"Listen, don't fall into that stereotype of good-looking women not knowing anything about their rides," I pitched her through the open driver's window as I gassed up her tank. "It's not about being a grease monkey. It's all high-tech now. Car mechanics is a science. If you want, I could come by your place and teach you some of the basics."

I didn't know how much of that rap I really believed. But it got me an afternoon alone with Melody in her driveway. Then a couple of movie dates after that, where I first slipped my arm around her, tasted those sweet lips, and took a walk with my hands as far as she'd let me.

Suddenly, every one of those girls on the bleachers began clapping over something.

"Thank you, ladies! Thank you!" yelled Bishop, without missing a beat. "I appreciate your worship!"

There were a few laughs from the bleachers, and even a sarcastic, "You're *not* welcome!"

Just then those girls started getting up to leave.

That's when Melody saw me, and began waving.

I bolted across the field towards her with the smell of the fresh-cut grass filling my lungs.

"Adonis, look up!" Ethan shouted, a second before he zipped me a pass.

I caught that pigskin in full stride and ran up to Melody with it tucked away beneath my left arm.

"So what's been going on here?" I asked her.

"First meeting of the Fashion Club," Melody answered with a wide pearly smile. "Big doings—we just elected officers."

"Oh, that's great," I said, trying to sound interested. "You know, lots of guys are into fashion, too. I know some of the most famous designers in the world are men."

"Yeah, you're right. They're some of my favorites—Ralph Lauren and Yves Saint Laurent. I'm pretty impressed you know that! Hey, I want you to meet someone," Melody said excitedly, reaching out to spin somebody around by the shoulder to face me. "Adonis, this is our new Fashion Club president, Alan."

· Everything inside me tensed up as my eyes locked onto his. That shrimp was almost a foot shorter than I was. And even standing on the bottom row of the bleachers, Alan was only eye level with me.

"Oh, yes. Hello," he said, flipping the tail end of a long scarf around his neck, like he was Snoopy that big-nosed dog from the Peanuts comics, ready to duel the Red Baron. "Adonis, you're in two of my classes, aren't you?"

It freaked me out that Alan knew that, like maybe he'd been watching my ass. Or even worse, he had some kind of man crush on me. But with Melody there, I was fighting back every instinct I had to snort at him.

"I'm not exactly sure," I answered.

"Well, it's a pleasure to *formally* meet you, Adonis," he said, extending his small pale hand. "Any friend of Melody's . . ."

I normally would have left a loser like him hanging out there. But I couldn't now. His grip felt so limp and clammy, I would have sworn I'd shoved my hand into a bowl of warm chowder.

"That's a very unusual name, Adonis," Alan said. "It comes from Greek mythology, doesn't it?"

I wasn't about to discuss anything *Greek* with Alan in public.

"Yeah, how did you get that name?" Melody asked.

"It was my mother's idea. She studied art, and there's some statue of a naked god with a perfect body named Adonis," I said, watching Melody look me over from head to toe. "My father liked it, too, because of his favorite wrestler growing up—Adorable Adrian Adonis, who was the tag-team champ."

That's when I heard a familiar voice call my name, and footsteps coming down the bleachers towards me.

"I believe you already know our vice president," Melody said.

I looked up and it was my sister Jeannie, who'd just become a junior.

"Since when do you care about fashion?" Jeannie asked, smirking from ear to ear. "I mean, besides what the cheerleaders are wearing?"

"I've got lots of interests you don't know about," I answered, with some attitude.

"Adonis, aren't you going to congratulate your sister?" Melody asked, nudging my elbow. "Vice president's a big honor, and *I* nominated her."

"Sure I am," I said. "Congratulations, Jeannie."

"Oh, she's a sweetheart, this one. She'll do a great job," Alan said.

Then he kissed Jeannie on the cheek, with a long *mmmmm-waa*, and that was enough for me.

"Hey, I gotta go. We're weight training today," I said, and turned my back to a chorus of good-byes.

The guys were all standing at the door to the trailer, grinning at me. And I could feel my face getting redder and redder on the walk over.

"You were pretty friendly with gay boy there," said Bishop, with the rest of them already laughing. "What he want from you?"

"Nothing. He wants a date with *you* after we're finished," I answered, tossing him the football. "I told him you'd definitely be into it."

———